The UNFORGETTABLE Tales of ADELINE BIGSBY

The Unwanted Alliance
Book 2

Elizabeth Mowery

Published by Wild & Free Publishing LLC, Tobaccoville, NC 27050

Library of Congress Control Number: 2025948097

ISBN: 979-8-9900151-2-8 (Paperback)

ISBN: 979-8-9900151-3-5 (eBook edition)

This is a work of fiction. Unless otherwise indicated, all the names, characters, businesses, places, events and incidents in this book are either the product of the author's imagination or used in a fictitious manner. Any resemblance to actual persons, living or dead, or actual events is purely coincidental.

Cover Design by Vivien Reis and Adam Mowery

To my incredible Mom, who believed in me long before I believed in myself.

Chapter One

"Happy birthday to you!"

Adeline Bigsby blew out the candles on her birthday cake as cheers erupted around the crowded patio. Her cheeks flushed as she smiled at the gathered family and friends, a gentle warmth blooming through her as colorful balloons swayed in the breeze.

Aunt Peggy and Uncle Pete had hosted Adeline's seventeenth birthday party at their home, and it couldn't have been more perfect. Twinkling lights hung over the pool and looped around the gazebo, casting a soft, enchanted glow across the backyard.

It was a perfect September day for a pool party.

Once the gifts were opened, the party fizzled out until only family remained. It didn't take long to clear away the paper plates and soda cans left behind.

"I think this is the last of the trash," Adeline said, stepping into the kitchen with a bulging garbage bag.

"Excellent." Uncle Pete took the heavy load from her. "I'll take care of it."

He disappeared into the garage, leaving Aunt Peggy and Mom to pack away the pizza boxes and chip bowls that covered every inch of counter space. Rebecca, Adeline's little sister, knelt beside a cooler, moving unopened sodas into the fridge.

"What else needs to be done?" Adeline asked, tucking her auburn waves behind her ears.

"We got it, sweetie," Aunt Peggy said, wiping her hands. "Go. Enjoy yourself."

"You sure?" Adeline asked. "I don't mind helping."

"Quite sure," Mom added, her voice gentle but distant. She forced a faint smile, but her eyes betrayed the emotion she was trying to bury.

Before Adeline could say more, her cousin Carol appeared and tugged her arm. "Come on!"

Carol dragged Adeline out the door, heading straight toward the hot tub. It had been a warm, sunny day, but it was getting chilly now that the vibrant moon had replaced the sun.

The cool air nipped at Adeline's nose as she dipped her legs into the bubbling water beside Carol. They had already changed out of their wet swimsuits, but Adeline was glad she'd grabbed her cardigan before Carol yanked her outside. The soft fabric slid across her chilly skin as she shoved her arms through the sleeves and wrapped herself in its warmth.

"That was such a fun party," Carol said.

"It really was."

Adeline's expression dimmed as she swirled her feet in the water. She'd had a good time, but she couldn't shake the trace of sadness that always crept in during holidays and big events.

"What's wrong?" Carol asked.

"I just wish my dad was here." Adeline shrugged as tears threatened to fall. "It doesn't feel right celebrating without him."

"I know." Carol wrapped an arm around Adeline's shoulders. "I wish he was here too."

They sat in silence, listening to the crickets and the water gurgling against their legs. The stillness lingered for a while.

"I'm really proud of you, Addie," Carol said as she withdrew her arm. "You've come a long way since the accident."

A tear slipped from Adeline's eye. She quickly wiped it away. "Thanks."

"And I, for one, am super glad you moved here."

Adeline cracked a small smile. "Me too."

Another wave of silence filled the night as tiny stars sparkled against the black backdrop. Adeline still couldn't believe she was about to hit the one-year mark of living in Black Mountain, North Carolina. It had been a whirlwind of surprises and challenges, but she was thankful for every twist and turn.

"You know what would have made your party even better?" Carol knocked Adeline from her thoughts.

"What?"

"If Jonathan McThorn had made a surprise visit."

Adeline let out a laugh and bumped shoulders with Carol. Jonathan McThorn had graduated from high school a few months earlier, but Adeline still had a major crush on him.

"I would've passed out," Adeline said.

"Oh, I know." Carol grinned. "He's still in town, you know. Didn't go off to college."

"Wait—what?" Adeline's eyebrows shot up.

"Yep. Took a job at his dad's real estate company."

"Are you serious?"

"Dead serious," Carol said. "Daniel's parents met with him last week."

"No way!"

"I swear." Carol laughed, clapping her hands together. "I found out today and couldn't wait to tell you."

Butterflies fluttered in Adeline's stomach. "I can't believe it."

"I can't either," Carol said, leaning back on her palms. "Now you can stare at him some more."

"Very funny." Adeline gave Carol a playful shove.

"I still can't believe you haven't spoken a word to him," Carol said. "We literally have tons of guy friends you talk to all the time."

"Yeah, but none of them look like Jonathan McThorn."

"You got a point there."

Adeline bit her lip, smiling. "Maybe one day I'll have the guts to speak to him."

"I hope so," Carol said. "But until then, you can enjoy the view."

She giggled. "Can't wait."

***

Sunday rolled around, kicking off the first day of October. It was fall, but the air still felt like summer as Adeline stepped outside in shorts and a T-shirt. It had been a week since she'd last crossed into the mysterious realm behind her house, and she was looking forward to seeing the friends who felt more like family.

Godfrey, Henry Snow, and Jesse lived in a cozy cabin tucked deep in the forest, and Adeline visited them often. She planned to stay a couple of days with them. No one in her world would even notice she was gone.

Time worked differently in that magical place. Whenever she stepped through the fence at the edge of her backyard, the world she left behind froze until she returned. She didn't age there, no matter how long she stayed, so she usually visited for a few days at a time.

The breeze lifted her long ponytail as she unlocked the rusted gate and stepped through, the old chain clinking softly behind her. It was hotter than she'd expected, but she had no complaints as she secured the door.

Leaving the key in the lock, Adeline made a beeline to a massive oak that towered over the other trees. She pushed aside the overgrown bush just enough to reach her hand inside the decaying log it hid.

The hidden space had become the ideal place for her to stash her weapon while she was away. She *never* brought the bizarre dagger into her world, fearing someone might see it. Or worse...steal it.

Adeline tapped her fingers along the earthy bottom until she felt the solid gold sheath that secured her dagger. She pulled it from the hiding place along with the leather belt it was attached to. Jesse had crafted it for her a while back. It made carrying her weapon much easier.

Adeline fastened the leather belt around her waist but stiffened when a twig snapped behind her.

Someone was there.

The footsteps were light—quiet and precise—but she heard them.

With lightning speed, Adeline drew her dagger from its sheath, raising the sharp tip toward the tall, lean figure moving through the trees.

It took only a second to recognize the familiar face just an arm's length away.

"Nice reflexes, Addie." Jesse grinned. "I'm impressed."

"You scared me!" Adeline lowered the blade, her heart still pounding. "How many times do I have to tell you not to sneak up on me?"

"It's part of your training," Jesse said, pulling her into a brief hug. "Got to keep you on your toes."

"I could've hurt you."

Jesse laughed and, with one smooth motion, plucked the blade from her hand. He pointed it at her chest. "Not a chance." He flipped the dagger once before handing it back.

"Point taken." Adeline tucked it away.

The hilt's jeweled top bounced against her hip as she fell in step beside Jesse. They followed the well-worn path beneath a ceiling of trees, golden light spilling through the branches. She couldn't tell what time of day it was. If she had to guess, she'd say mid-morning.

It had taken Adeline a while to get used to the different seasons in that realm since they rarely matched the ones in her world. It could be the dead of winter in her backyard, only to feel like the middle of summer as soon as she stepped past the barrier separating the two worlds. The mysterious forest always disguised itself from the outside world, so she never knew what to expect.

More often than not, she found herself unprepared for the weather shift and had to return home to change clothes. But not today. She couldn't have picked a better outfit.

"What do you want to do today?" Adeline asked.

"We've got to complete our workout before doing anything else," Jesse said, his wavy chestnut hair bouncing down his back.

"Since it's my birthday weekend, I was hoping we could take the day off."

"Good try," Jesse said. "But no."

Adeline groaned. "Come on. We literally work out *every* time I'm here."

"It's good for you," Jesse replied with an infectious grin. "Now. Enough of this whining. Let's knock out today's lesson."

"Fine." Adeline rolled her eyes. "Let's get this over with."

Chapter Two

The blazing sun beat down on Adeline as she pulled back the bowstring of her recurve bow, her fingers touching the corner of her mouth. Sweat dripped down her back, and her muscles burned as she aimed the arrow at the target more than twenty-five yards away. Her limbs ached, but her stance was steady as she locked onto the bullseye.

"A little higher," Jesse said, hovering behind her.

Adeline tilted the bow upward before releasing the tight string.

Zoom!

The arrow smashed into the center of the target, spraying hay into the air.

"Great job!" Jesse patted her on the back.

"Thanks," she said, lowering her bow. "I think I'm finally getting the hang of it."

"I'd say."

A smile tugged at Adeline's lips. She'd come a long way since her first training lesson with Jesse.

Before moving to Black Mountain, she'd thought Dad had been hard on her. But he had nothing on Jesse. Most days, it felt like she'd joined the military. She'd lost count of how many times she'd vomited after drills or collapsed during an endless run through the garden.

The workouts were brutal, but she was in the best shape of her life.

All thanks to Jesse.

"Get some water." Jesse swiped a hand across his sweaty brows. "We're not quite done yet."

Groaning, Adeline slung her recurve bow over her shoulder before reaching for her water bottle. Her ponytail was soaked with sweat, as was her outfit.

She took a quick swig of water before squeezing the bottle over her head. Cold water splashed onto her auburn hair and rolled down her cheeks, cooling her flushed skin.

"What now?" Adeline rubbed the water from her eyes.

"We're going to work on your combat."

"Combat?" Adeline grumbled, tossing the empty bottle to the grass. "My arms are going to fall off."

Jesse chuckled. "You're so dramatic."

Adeline gave him an eye roll as they moved to the only building in the training space. He was just as sweaty as she was, but he didn't complain as he lifted the hem of his T-shirt and wiped his trimmed beard.

They'd been out in the heat for two hours straight. That wasn't unusual, but Adeline was ready to call it a day. All she could think about was relaxing at the cabin as she entered the metal building with bare walls and a cement floor. It looked like a big, empty storage unit.

The blinding lights flicked on as soon as their motion was detected, and so did the much-needed air conditioning. Adeline closed her eyes as cold air blasted against her hot skin.

"We're almost done." Jesse closed the door behind him. "I promise."

"I hate this so much," she said, not even bothering to look his way.

"Oh, I know. But you'll thank me for it one day."

Jesse went to activate the program. Having seen it so many times, Adeline was no longer fazed by the futuristic hologram that appeared on the wall every time Jesse scanned his palm. A giant keyboard made of light hovered before them, but she paid it no attention.

"You'll be using your dagger this time," Jesse said, typing away on the bright keys.

Adeline leaned her bow against the door and pulled her quiver over her head. After placing it on the ground, she rolled her aching shoulders and grasped the dagger resting at her side.

A dull ache throbbed in her arm as she examined the dagger she'd found in Loydaya. Tiny sparkles of light danced inside the glass blade—beautiful and mesmerizing. It barely weighed a thing, but she felt like she'd just picked up a sledgehammer.

"What am I going to kill now?" Adeline asked. "A warthog? A bear?"

"We're switching it up this time." Jesse tapped the final key.

In a flash, the room changed.

Holding a hand up to the blinding sun, Adeline went still. They were standing in the middle of a massive arena. It reminded her of the Colosseum in Rome, where gladiators fought to the death. But they were not alone.

The hot, dry air vibrated with excitement from the rowdy crowd that packed the stands. Adeline's stomach knotted as she did a slow spin. There wasn't an empty seat in sight.

Normally, she trained in outdoor settings like a forest or a desert. Never in a place like this and *never* with spectators.

"Where are we?" she asked, her voice shaky.

"A stadium," he said, scanning the sea of people. "It's perfect for what I have planned."

A holographic opponent appeared in the center of the dusty arena, and Adeline stopped breathing.

The man standing before her was bald, enormous, and fully outfitted in black tactical gear. He was built like a brick house. Easily three times her size.

She moved back, planting herself beside Jesse. She'd only practiced with animals, never humans. "Who is that?"

"This is one of Ralock's warriors," Jesse said, nodding toward the man who was stockier than him.

Adeline stood rigid. She knew little about Ralock and his military. "They're really that big?"

"They come in all sizes," he said. "But if you can handle the biggest, the rest will be easy."

Adeline gulped and looked up at the towering man.

"Come on." Jesse gave the middle of her sweaty back a push, nudging her forward. "Face your opponent."

Reluctantly, Adeline took a step. The warrior didn't move—just stared straight ahead like a statue. He was even bigger up close. Veins bulged along his biceps as sweat trickled down his temples in the heat.

She had to remind herself that he wasn't real, but her heart still fluttered like crazy. Her sore muscles were now the last thing on her mind. The man was a beast. He didn't have a weapon, but she was positive his fists could punch a hole through her.

"All the warriors usually have weapons, but I didn't give this guy one," Jesse said. "I want you to get used to fighting someone bigger than you without worrying about a weapon."

"That's so thoughtful of you," Adeline said with a touch of sarcasm.

"I know." Jesse grinned as he stepped aside. "Now get in front of him."

Adeline shuffled forward, stopping before the biggest man she had ever seen. She tightened her grip on her dagger, bracing herself for the fight.

"Ready!" Jesse called, triggering the opponent.

The warrior's eyes locked onto hers. Cold and unblinking. Then he struck like a viper. His fist slammed into her stomach before she could react, knocking her to the dusty ground.

Pain blasted through Adeline as she rolled onto her side, clutching her stomach. She tried to breathe through the sharp ache as the crowd thundered in her ears. They didn't care about her pain. They just shouted with excitement, cheering for her opponent.

"That hurt," she moaned.

The fans kept chanting, and Adeline silently hoped Jesse would call it quits.

"Come on. You've got this, Addie." Jesse hauled her up. "Use your speed. Dodge his punches and go for the neck."

Adeline groaned as she faced the warrior again. His lifeless eyes watched her as he stood motionless. She was glad he hadn't hit her while she was down. Jesse must've programmed him that way.

Jesse took a few steps back. "He'll fight back when you make the first move."

Adeline gave her arms a quick shake and lunged forward. The warrior jumped back, avoiding the sharp blade aimed at his throat. He came at her full force, swinging hard. She dove to the side, rolled into a somersault, and sprang to her feet.

He wound back his fist, and Adeline swung her dagger at his neck. But her aim was slightly off. The glass blade slashed across his breastplate, burning through his thick armor. Sparks of electricity crackled inside the open wound as the warrior stumbled back, roaring with rage.

While he was distracted, Adeline went in for the kill.

She charged, dagger raised—but just as she struck, the warrior snatched her wrist. In one swift motion, he yanked her off the ground. She dangled in the air, kicking and screaming as his iron knuckles hammered into her side.

Agony exploded in her ribcage as the warrior dropped her hard on her back. He faced the crowd with raised arms, shouting obscenities. The fans went wild. Their shouts reverberated through the stadium, shaking the ground beneath Adeline as she stared up at the blue sky.

Her ribs throbbed as she hugged her side, waiting for Jesse to turn off the simulator. She'd already taken two nasty blows. Surely, he could see she wasn't ready to face someone that strong.

"Again!" Jesse called out.

"Again?" Adeline jerked her head his way. "Are you trying to kill me?"

Jesse crossed his arms, giving her a look. "The only way you'll get stronger is if I push you."

"Push me to my death?"

"Get up, Addie. You're not a quitter."

"I can't." She closed her eyes, still sprawled across the arena floor. "He's too big."

"Now!"

"Ugh." Adeline slammed her fist against the ground, then forced herself to stand.

Pain pulsed in her ribs as she steadied herself, wiping the sweat from her brow. The crowd booed. Her lips flattened as she scanned the nameless faces jeering at her.

Heavy boots pounded against the ground. Adeline turned and froze.

The warrior didn't wait for her to start the fight. He was coming right at her.

Adeline leaped to the side, avoiding his fist. He threw a left hook, then a right hook—again and again. She moved from side to side, dodging the powerful punches, but she was wearing out fast.

Another solid swing came, nailing her hard in the stomach.

She collapsed to her knees as pain knifed across her ribs. Doubling over, she held her aching stomach, gasping for air.

A malicious laugh rumbled from the warrior as he raised his arms to the crowd. He pumped his fists triumphantly, and the people went berserk. Their cheers pounded into Adeline's skull as she lifted her head, struggling to catch her breath.

The roar didn't let up as the warrior turned to Adeline with an arrogant smirk. "Fight me, girl."

Adeline shook her head while sucking in a lungful of air.

"I said *fight me!*"

The warrior strutted toward Adeline, dust billowing from his boots. Panic flooded her body, but she was too weak to move.

Jesse cut in front of Adeline and slammed his hands into the warrior's chest. The force sent him stumbling back, but he quickly regained his balance. His features hardened as he clenched his fist and swung at Jesse.

The punch sliced through empty air as Jesse ducked just in time—missing him by inches. He pivoted and launched his own fist into the warrior's temple with a loud crack.

The sound of bones breaking split the air as the warrior collapsed to the ground with a heavy thump. A hush fell on the crowd as Jesse stood over him. He drew his longsword from his hip and plunged the tip into the enemy's chest. It pierced the thick breastplate, and the hologram slowly faded away.

The crowd erupted into a thunderous celebration, chanting Jesse's name repeatedly.

"And that's how it's done." Jesse slid his sword back into its sheath.

"Show-off," she said, the corner of her lip lifting.

Jesse flashed Adeline a smile as he offered her a hand. She grabbed it, and he pulled her to her feet. Pain shot through her.

"Off!" Jesse yelled.

As soon as the word left his mouth, the lively crowd and the arena vanished. Only the empty room remained. The blast of air conditioning hit Adeline as she stashed her dagger and wiped her dusty, sweat-soaked clothes the best she could.

"I'm proud of you," Jesse said, retrieving her bow and quiver and handing them over. "You did really well today."

"I just got the crap beat out of me." Adeline shouldered her quiver before grabbing her recurve bow.

"That lesson was meant to toughen you up," Jesse said. "Once you're used to fighting warriors, nothing will scare you."

"If you say so." Adeline pushed the door and hobbled into the heat. "I'm pretty sure that dude broke my ribs."

"He didn't," Jesse said as they walked out of the training area. "But you'll have a nasty bruise tomorrow."

"Nothing new."

"I know you don't always understand why I'm so hard on you," Jesse said, his tone turning serious. "But it's necessary for what's ahead. This realm can be very dangerous."

"I know that, Jesse." Adeline wiped her sweaty face with her sleeve. "I still have that scar from Ralock."

Saying his name made her throat go dry. Ralock was the vilest being in that realm. He looked like a man, but he was a wicked beast who had nearly taken her life.

"Ralock isn't the only one who can harm you," Jesse said. "There are many deadly creatures here, and they'll kill you if you're not ready."

Adeline sighed as they crossed over the stone bridge, the garden unfolding around them in vibrant beauty. She hadn't seen anything dangerous since Ralock. That had been almost a year ago.

After fighting Ralock in the Loydaya tunnel, Adeline had been frightened to go anywhere alone. She'd begged her friends to stay close, and they had. They met her when she arrived, walked with her to the cabin, and made sure she got home safely.

Over time, her confidence had returned. She no longer needed them to babysit her. She knew the forest well and had memorized the paths to the cabin. Walking them alone didn't leave her on edge anymore, especially now that she was comfortable with her weapons.

Adeline still found joy and beauty in the vast forest and garden, but she often wondered what the other territories were like. Were they like her world, full of shops and homes? What were the people like?

She didn't want to only hear about them; she wanted to see them for herself.

Now at seventeen, Adeline felt ready to see what else was out there.

"Is that why you haven't shown me the other territories?" she asked Jesse.

"Yes. A lot of places here aren't safe." Jesse's sword tapped against his thigh as he walked. "Remember, if you die here, time keeps moving in your world. Your family and friends would never know what happened to you."

Adeline's stomach rolled. Her thoughts went to Mom and her little sister, Rebecca. She still didn't have a close relationship with either of them, but they would be devastated if she disappeared without a trace. They'd already endured the shocking death of her father. She could never put them through that again.

"When will I be ready?" Adeline asked, the pain in her ribs reawakening with every step.

"Soon." Jesse bumped her shoulder lightly with his. "Very soon."

Chapter Three

Adeline stepped out of the shower, feeling like a brand-new person. She changed into a comfy outfit from the magical dresser that produced any clothing she desired. Facing the mirror, she wrung the towel through her wet hair, then combed her fingers through the long, wavy strands. Even the simplest task made her arms ache. She gave up before all the knots were out.

Curious to see the damage from training, Adeline lifted her T-shirt and cringed. Yellow bruises marked her stomach. They already hurt—and tomorrow would be worse—but she didn't dwell on it. She was used to being achy and sore, especially after tough days with Jesse.

Adeline let her shirt fall and smoothed her damp hair back behind her ears. She smiled at her reflection before turning to leave. The scent of birch wood still lingered from the stone fireplace as she passed it and rounded her favorite loveseat.

After spending so much time in that bedroom over the past year, she'd claimed it as her own. She was certain she'd slept there more than in her actual bedroom back in Black Mountain, but she never stayed longer than a week at a time. Eleventh grade had just started, and she couldn't afford to fall behind.

She still hadn't told anyone about the hidden realm. Not even her cousin Carol, who usually knew everything. The mystical forest behind her house was her secret, and she planned on keeping it that way.

As Adeline stepped into the wide hallway, a delicious smell hit her. By the time she reached the kitchen, the air was rich with the scent of chocolate chip cookies. Her jolly old friend, Henry Snow, was pulling a tray from the oven.

Just seeing him made her grin. Henry had become like a grandfather to her and was the reason she'd ended up there in the first place.

"Just in time!" Henry said, placing the baking sheet on the stove to cool.

Adeline leaned against the counter. "It smells amazing, like always."

"Just wait until you taste one."

Adeline didn't need a bite to know they'd be good. Henry was always in the kitchen, whipping up something tasty. Food could magically appear there, but Henry preferred to make everything from scratch, and it was always phenomenal.

"This is for you, love." Henry handed Adeline a cold bottle of water from the fridge.

"Thanks, Henry."

Adeline twisted off the cap and took a quick sip. The cold liquid was crisp as it rolled down her dry throat. Even the water in the cabin tasted better than anything in her world.

"Sit." Henry gestured to the barstool at the island. "I want to hear all about your training."

"Well..." Adeline winced as she carefully sat down. "Jesse thought it'd be a great idea to introduce me to one of Ralock's warriors today."

"Did he now?" Henry's white mustache twitched as he chuckled. "How did that go?"

"Not good. He nearly killed me."

"Nonsense." He waved his wrinkled hand through the air. "Jesse would never allow that."

"It sure felt like it. I've never been hit that hard before."

"Just wait until tomorrow," Jesse said, strolling in from the hallway. His damp hair waved down his back as he headed straight for the cookies. He plucked one from the tray and took a bite. "Not bad, old man."

Henry playfully smacked Jesse's arm before grabbing a cookie for himself. Jesse looked to be in his early twenties, but he was best friends with Henry, who was well over seventy. They were always teasing each other.

"Do you want one, Addie?" Jesse pointed to the tray.

Steam rolled from the freshly made treats, but Adeline wasn't hungry. Hours in the blazing sun had killed her appetite. She shook her head. "I'll stick with water for now."

Jesse grabbed another one. "You're missing out."

"I'll have some later," Adeline said, taking another drink.

"You'd better," Henry teased.

"When is Godfrey coming back?" Adeline asked. "I feel like he's been gone forever."

Godfrey was Jesse's father and the one who had helped her cope with the tragic loss of her dad. He'd become the father figure she so desperately needed.

"He's on his way back as we speak," Henry said cheerfully.

Adeline hadn't seen Godfrey in weeks. He'd been away on some unknown journey, and she was more than ready for him to come home.

"I think I may have heard something outside." Henry grinned, deepening his wrinkles. "You should probably check the garden."

Adeline shot off the barstool and nearly tripped over herself as she raced out the backdoor, not even bothering to close it behind her.

Humidity smacked her as she stepped onto the porch, the heat burning her bare feet. She shaded her eyes from the sun and scanned the garden that stretched endlessly before her.

Cherry blossoms danced in the breeze, their petals spiraling slowly to the path below, while butterflies and bumblebees moved lazily from flower to flower. The whole garden seemed alive, breathing with color and sound. The beauty was breathtaking, almost unreal. But something else caught her breath.

A heavyset man was strolling toward her. His bushy red hair bounced as his face split into a grand smile.

It was Godfrey.

Chapter Four

"Hello, Addie." Godfrey waved.

"You're back!" Adeline dashed down the steps and sprinted into the garden, crashing into Godfrey's open arms. His jolly laughter filled her ears as he squeezed her tight and lifted her up before setting her back on her feet. "I've missed you."

"And I've missed you." Godfrey tapped the tip of her nose. "It's been way too long."

"Seriously," she said. "How was your trip?"

"It went well." Godfrey draped a thick arm around her shoulders and walked her toward the cabin. "I'm just glad to be back."

"Me too."

Adeline couldn't stop smiling as she soaked in Godfrey's presence. It was like liquid love. Warmth pooled in her stomach as she strolled next to him. She could never quite explain it, but Godfrey was special. He always made her feel better. All she had to do was be near him to absorb his peace.

Once they stepped into the cool cabin, Jesse and Henry swarmed Godfrey. They nearly tackled him in their excitement.

"It's wonderful to have you back, Godfrey," Henry said, his brown eyes shining. "You must tell us how the journey went."

Godfrey pulled out a chair at the dining table and dropped into it with a lingering grin. As everyone gathered around, his expression grew solemn. He leaned back, folding his hands atop his round belly. "My trip to Blistering Heights was a success, but it was hard to see what's happening there."

"Blistering Heights?" Adeline's face scrunched. "What's that?"

"A small region in the northeast," Jesse explained.

"Oh." She turned back to Godfrey. "Why'd you go there?"

"Our friends there asked to meet with me."

"Why?"

"Ralock's military has been raiding their village, and they need help," Godfrey said. "We've put some security in place, but it won't be enough. The threat needs to be eliminated."

A cold weight settled over Adeline as she sank back into her seat. She'd only seen Ralock's army once and still had nightmares about it.

"I'll do it." Jesse raised his hand. "I could use the practice."

"I figured you would," Godfrey said, his tone steady with approval.

Adeline's pulse spiked. One warrior had nearly taken her out. How was Jesse supposed to face an entire army?

"You can't go alone," Adeline blurted.

"Who said I was?" Jesse asked.

Adeline glanced around the table. She'd never seen Henry or Godfrey use a weapon. Surely Jesse didn't mean them.

"You two are going?" she asked, looking between them.

"No." Godfrey shook his head. "Henry and I will head south to deal with something else."

She frowned. "Then who are you going with, Jesse?"

"You."

"*Me?*"

"Yep." Jesse dipped his bearded chin. "You've been wanting to explore our realm. Here's your chance."

"I meant traveling. Seeing other places. Not going on a killing spree," she said, her words tumbling out in a rush.

"It'll be good for you."

"Absolutely not." She crossed her arms. "I'm not going."

"That's your choice," Jesse said with a shrug, "but it will be the adventure of a lifetime."

"I'm not ready to fight Ralock's warriors. I barely survived one today."

"You're ready," Jesse said, his green eyes reassuring.

"No, I'm not."

"He's right, Addie," Godfrey said gently. "It's time to put all that training to good use."

Adeline's stomach turned. The grueling hours of training she'd endured over the past year came rushing back. Blazing heat, icy wind, pouring rain: nothing ever postponed Jesse's workouts. Day after day, she had pushed through the pain and misery, thinking it was all for self-defense. Clearly not.

"You won't know what you're capable of until you step out of your comfort zone," Godfrey said.

Adeline scrambled for another excuse. Nothing came to mind. "I can't fight warriors, Godfrey," she said, placing a hand on her aching side. "I've only trained with animals."

"You can, Addie." Godfrey beamed, the small gap between his front teeth peeking through. "Trust me."

Confidence and mischief sparkled in Godfrey's crystal blue eyes; it was clear he knew something she didn't. And strangely, just looking at him stirred a spark of excitement deep within her.

She'd always longed to explore new places. Now was her chance.

Adeline swallowed hard, a thousand doubts pounding inside her. And yet...the pull to say yes was stronger than the fear holding her back.

"All right." She huffed. "I'll go."

"You won't regret it." Thin wrinkles creased at the corners of Godfrey's eyes as his grin deepened. "We'll be in constant communication with you, so there's no need to worry."

Adeline gave a small nod, a hint of amusement tugging at her mouth. She loved that she could talk to each of them telepathically at any time. Even in her world.

"When do we head out?" Jesse asked Godfrey.

"Tomorrow morning, after a good night's sleep."

"Sounds good." Jesse stood. "I'll start organizing and packing the supplies."

"And I'll start dinner." Henry went into the kitchen.

Adeline stayed glued to her seat, picking at her nails.

What if I get hurt? she wondered. *Or get separated from Jesse? What if we run out of supplies?*

"You don't need to be afraid," Godfrey said, snapping her from her thoughts.

"What if something bad happens to me?"

"Fear will always try to keep you from your destiny," he said, meeting her gaze across the table.

"Can I go with you instead?"

"No, you need to go with Jesse." Godfrey patted her hand before rising from his seat. His hefty body shuffled toward Henry, who was already chopping vegetables. Laughter broke out between them, but Adeline tuned it out.

Her focus drifted to the window. *What have I gotten myself into?*

Chapter Five

The rising sun spilled through the bedroom window as birds greeted the morning with pleasant chirps. Adeline lay asleep, curled beneath a feathery comforter that nearly swallowed her whole.

"Addie," Godfrey whispered, giving her a little shake. "Wake up."

She groaned, her eyes fluttering open to find Godfrey and Henry standing over her.

"We're leaving and wanted to say goodbye," Henry said, his warm smile crinkling his eyes.

Adeline hugged them both, her sore stomach aching with each embrace. "Bye."

"We will talk soon," Henry assured her.

They gave a final wave before slipping out and closing the door. Adeline leaned back against the headboard and shut her eyes. Every inch of her body begged for more sleep, but she fought against it. Kicking off the covers, she stood with a stretch. Pain flared in her ribs, but it wasn't unbearable.

She yawned as she made her way to the dresser and changed into jean shorts and a tank top before throwing her bedhead into a messy bun. A few strands escaped, but she didn't bother taming them as she shoved her feet into her favorite sneakers and grabbed her quiver.

A ripple of discomfort ran down her arm as she placed the quiver over her head, tightening the strap at her chest. Next, she attached her dagger to her hip and grabbed her bow before exiting the room.

The cabin was deathly quiet as she stepped into the main area.

No sign of Jesse.

Movement beyond the window drew her gaze. He was in the front yard with their horses, Regal and Angela. She'd seen them countless times, but their beauty never ceased to amaze her.

Regal was Jesse's trusted steed. He was solid black and all muscle, with navy highlights flowing through his mane and tail. He was as fierce as he looked. No one in their right mind would mess with him.

Angela, on the other hand, looked like she'd galloped out of a fairytale. Her sleek white coat shimmered in the light, and lavender streaks glimmered through her hair. Jesse had given her to Adeline the year before, and she'd been in love with her ever since.

Soreness tugged at Adeline as she stepped outside. The heavy humidity hit her like a wall, wrapping her in sticky heat. It would be another hot day.

"There she is." Jesse greeted her with a grin as he tightened the strap on Regal's saddle. Sweat beaded along his hairline, soaking into the messy bun that looked just as wild as hers. "I was just about to wake you up."

"Godfrey and Henry beat you to it," she said, descending the steps.

"You almost ready?" Jesse asked, swiping sweat from his face. "We've got a long journey ahead of us."

"Yeah, I'm ready."

Adeline went straight to Angela. The horse pranced in place like a show horse, eager and full of energy.

"Good morning, sweet girl," Adeline said, rubbing under her chin.

Angela neighed in reply.

"Someone's excited to see you," Jesse said as he climbed onto Regal, his sword bouncing against his thigh as he settled into the saddle.

Grinning, Adeline secured her bow on the saddle beside the large leather bag stuffed to the brim. "Why'd you pack so much?" she asked as she mounted Angela and got situated.

"We'll be gone for a few days."

"What?" Adeline nearly choked. "I thought this was a day trip."

"Blistering Heights isn't close, Addie." Jesse tossed her a quick glance. "It'll take us a couple of days to get there."

"Where are we going to sleep?"

"Under the stars."

Uneasiness expanded within Adeline. She loved the outdoors but had little experience with camping. Especially in such a dangerous world.

"You're going to need this today," Jesse said, tossing her a small tube.

Adeline caught it. "What is it?"

"Sunscreen."

The smell of cucumbers penetrated the air as Adeline squeezed the light cream into her palms and rubbed it over her fair skin.

"Thanks." She tossed it back to him.

"No problem," Jesse said, snatching it midair and tucking it into his backpack. "That should last you the whole trip."

Jesse nudged his boots into Regal's sides, and Angela followed. They maneuvered around the vibrant flowerbeds and trees that filled the yard before entering the lively forest. The horses' hooves clapped against the dry ground as they moved along the worn path, startling a squirrel that darted up a nearby tree.

They rode in silence as streaks of sunlight broke through the branches above. It wasn't long before they reached a fork in the road. One led west, the other east. Adeline knew exactly where they were. The western trail would take her home; she wasn't sure where the other would lead.

Jesse chose the unknown path.

Nerves sparked in Adeline as she trotted behind him, the warm breeze caressing her face. She should be excited about exploring new territories, but the thought of fighting warriors smothered that feeling.

Every snap of a twig or rustle in the brush sent her heart racing, the tension mounting with each passing second.

After a while, the trees gave way, and the horses stepped onto a steep cliff overlooking a vast valley of red poppies.

Adeline pulled hard on the reins, her breath catching in her throat.

The Dark Territory.

The delicate flowers swayed in the wind, and so did the trees that covered the towering mountain. It was stunning, but she didn't want to be anywhere near it.

"You can't be serious." Adeline stiffened in the saddle. "You want to go through Ralock's land?"

"We're not going in there," Jesse said, steering Regal away from the cliff. "There's another route to Blistering Heights."

"Okay, good." Tension eased from her shoulders. "You almost gave me a heart attack."

They ventured onward, the temperature rising as they jumped from path to path. Before long, the forest began to change. The thick trees thinned, and the dirt trail turned to sand and scattered pebbles.

"Whoa." Jesse pulled on the reins, stopping Regal in his tracks.

Adeline did the same, her heart picking up speed. Dust clouded her vision for only a second. When it cleared, her stomach dropped.

The path went straight down, leading to an endless desert with a reddish-orange hue. Most of the trees were replaced by jagged rocks and misshaped boulders that seemed to scrape the sky. The dry, rocky landscape looked like another world, harsh and unwelcoming.

Adeline shielded her eyes from the sun. "Is this Blistering Heights?"

"Nope. This is the Red-Rock Region," Jesse said, squinting against the sunlight.

Adeline scanned the unfamiliar terrain. It didn't have an end. "How are we supposed to get down there?"

"Our horses can handle this path."

Adeline glanced down. The drop was at least fifty feet. "Are you sure?"

"Positive," he said, kicking his heels into Regal. "Take your time and hold on tight."

Regal stepped forward and zipped down the steep, rocky trail. Pebbles and rocks tumbled beneath his hooves as he slid downward, gaining speed. A moment later, they were safely on solid ground.

Once the dust cleared, Jesse waved her down. "Come on, Addie."

Adeline gnawed on her bottom lip as she squeezed the reins. "Let's go, Angela."

Angela approached the edge and plunged downward. Dust billowed from her hooves as they whizzed down the slope. The wind slapped Adeline's face as she held on for dear life. She was still shaking even after they reached the bottom.

"Good job." Jesse tossed her a quick grin.

The rocky desert was relatively flat and looked even larger now that Adeline was in it. Cactuses and other dry shrubs dotted the arid landscape, scattered among barren trees and enormous boulders.

As she took in the sunbaked land, something odd caught her eye. To her far left stood a dense batch of evergreens. They were thick and stout, planted in a straight line.

"What's in there?" Adeline pointed to the trees.

Jesse looked that way. "That area connects to the forest near the cabin, and to the northern part of the Dark Territory."

Adeline cringed. She desperately hoped they wouldn't run into Ralock on their journey.

Pulling her eyes from the evergreens, she held a hand to the scorching sun. "How long will we be in this desert?"

Jesse's hand shot up, signaling her to be quiet.

She went still, every muscle drawing tight. A trickle of sweat slid down her face as she searched the open desert. No movement. No sound. Only the heavy sense that something was watching.

A deafening roar ripped through the air.

Adeline's soul leaped from her body as a massive grizzly bear stomped out from behind a nearby boulder. It stood on its hind legs and gnashed its teeth, drool spraying from its mouth.

For a split second, she was paralyzed until her training kicked in. Adrenaline surged through her veins as she snatched her bow. Her hands fumbled for an arrow, but before she could nock it—

Jesse's arrow struck the grizzly between the eyes. It staggered, then crashed face-first into the ground. The earth shook as its body went still.

Adeline lowered her bow in disbelief. His speed and aim were flawless.

Jesse slid off Regal and approached the bear. He nudged it with his boot. "It's dead, all right."

Adeline's hands were shaking as she urged Angela forward. "I can't believe you killed it with one arrow."

"Shooting anything between the eyes will do the trick," he said, a grin tugging at his lips.

"True." Adeline smiled back, slipping her bow back into its place.

Sweat dripped from Jesse's beard as he did a quick sweep of the area. The coast was clear. He climbed back onto Regal and led the way through the open, dusty terrain.

"I'm glad you heard that bear," Adeline said, riding beside him. "I had no idea it was there."

"Me too," Jesse said. "He was waiting for us."

"How did he know we were coming?"

"He could smell us."

A shiver crawled up Adeline's spine. She'd battled bears in the combat simulator before, but this was different. She was out in the wild and no longer had the luxury of turning off the simulator if things got out of hand. She had to fight whether she was ready or not.

What else is out here?

CHAPTER SIX

THE TEMPERATURE HAD COOLED now that the sun had dipped behind a mountainous boulder. They had ridden nonstop, and Adeline was ready for it to end. Her legs ached, and her bottom was numb. The ongoing jarring hadn't helped the bruises on her stomach either.

"Let's camp here," Jesse said, hopping off his stallion and leading him between a cluster of boulders until they were out of sight.

Adeline slid off Angela, leaving streaks of red dust on her mare's side. Being back on solid ground felt good. She stretched her stiff legs and went after Jesse, Angela trotting close behind.

Jesse was already unpacking supplies when Adeline entered their makeshift campsite. It was nothing more than a small, circular space enclosed by looming rocks. The only way out was the way they'd come in.

At least we aren't sleeping out in the open, she told herself.

Adeline unclipped her sleeping bag from Angela's saddle and dropped it to the ground. She did the same with her backpack, surprised by its weight.

Opening the flap, Adeline squatted and began digging through it, her thighs burning from the strain. The pack was so full that it was hard to get her hand inside. Matches, food, extra clothing: Jesse had packed everything she could possibly need.

"I'll grab some firewood," Jesse said, heading for the exit.

Adeline stood. "I'll come with you."

"Stay with the horses." He paused at the entrance, turning back to her. "I'll be right back."

Adeline watched him leave, anxiety creeping up her throat. It would be dark soon.

What if he doesn't come back?

Shoving the thought away, she glanced at Regal and Angela. They were munching on a nearby shrub, too preoccupied with their snack to notice Jesse's absence. At least she wasn't completely alone.

Letting out a slow breath, Adeline slipped her quiver off and set it beside her backpack. She rolled her sore shoulders and tried using her fingers to release some of the tension. It didn't help.

Keeping her dagger strapped to her hip, she unrolled the sleeping bag on the dry ground and scouted the area for creepy-crawlies. She'd seen more than enough scorpions and tarantulas for one day.

She searched high and low, spotting a few bugs here and there. Nothing poisonous.

Hopefully nothing crawls into my sleeping bag.

Next, she gathered rocks and began building a firepit. She took her time selecting ones that weren't too heavy, arranging them in a circle between the sleeping bags.

Pleased with her work, she brushed the dust from her hands and looked toward the entrance. Jesse was nowhere in sight.

"Where are you?" Adeline asked Jesse telepathically.

"I'm almost done." His voice bounced inside her mind.

A loud groan from her stomach reminded her just how hungry she was. She'd had a few snacks throughout the day, but the heat had dulled her appetite. She went back to her backpack and rummaged through it, grabbing the first thing she saw: a pack of peanuts. She plopped down on her sleeping bag and tore open the package. Pouring a handful into her palm, she popped a few peanuts into her mouth. The salty treat hit the spot.

Seconds felt like minutes, and Adeline jumped at every sound. Coyotes howled in the distance, while rodents scurried for food. She wasn't usually so skittish, but every little noise sent a wave of fear through her. The longer she waited, the worse it got.

The sun was nearly gone. Jesse still hadn't returned. Where was he?

A flicker of motion at the entrance jolted Adeline upright. Her hand flew to her dagger, then lowered.

It was Jesse, his arms loaded with sticks.

"Awesome firepit." He dumped the sticks into the circle. "I couldn't have done it better myself."

Jesse arranged the wood into a neat pile, struck a match, and tossed it into the pit. The dry sticks lit instantly. He fanned the flames until they crackled and spread.

The sun sank quickly, and within minutes, the sky was black and blanketed with countless stars. The flames popped and danced against the dark backdrop while Adeline and Jesse ate a simple dinner of dried meat and fruit.

The steady pop and hiss of the fire should've been calming to Adeline as she finished her last bite, yet nothing could silence her racing mind. What if another bear showed up while they slept? Or a group of warriors?

"You're awfully quiet," Jesse said, watching her through the flames.

Adeline hugged her knees to her chest. "I don't like this place."

"Most people don't. It's way too hot."

"And dangerous."

"That too."

"It's also dusty," she added. "And there are tons of scorpions."

"Don't forget about the snakes."

"Can't forget about those." A half-smile played on her lips. "This place is a real gem."

"It sure is." Jesse let out a deep laugh. "Aren't you glad you came with me?"

As if on cue, a nearby coyote let out a chilling howl. Adeline tensed, gripping her weapon. More coyotes joined in, creating an eerie ensemble that echoed across the rocky terrain. Her heart pounded, and her grip tightened. Then they stopped.

She shot Jesse a fearful look.

"Those coyotes won't bother us," Jesse said, the firelight illuminating his plain features.

"It's not just that." She let go of the dagger's hilt. "I hate this place. Everything about it is terrifying."

Jesse looked at her, his green eyes steady. "I've prepared you for this journey."

"Then why am I so afraid?"

"Because you're out in the wild and don't know what to expect."

Adeline looked away, her chest still pumping as the fire cast strange shadows along the rocks. She couldn't remember the last time she'd felt such fear, and she hated it. All she wanted was the comfort of the cabin. She never should've left.

"Time for some shuteye." Jesse kicked off his boots and set them aside. "We've got another long day tomorrow."

Jesse got himself settled for the night, and Adeline did the same. She kept her sneakers close, and her dagger closer, as she crawled into her sleeping bag. The hard, rocky ground offered little relief to her weary body, but she was too tired to care.

Crickets chirped a soft melody as Adeline closed her eyes. A whirlwind of thoughts crowded her mind. She fought to quiet them, but they only intensified. Finally, exhaustion dragged her into a deep, dreamless sleep.

CHAPTER SEVEN

ADELINE SPRANG AWAKE TO the sound of squawking birds. She sat up, drenched in sweat, her heart pounding as hawks circled overhead. Not the alarm clock she was expecting.

Stupid birds.

She flopped back down, nestling into her sleeping bag. She drifted back to sleep, only to be reawakened by the smell of a campfire.

"Time to get up," Jesse said, his voice chipper. "We've got to move if we want to stay on track."

She rolled over, facing the other way. "Five more minutes."

"Get up." Jesse circled the fire and gave her shoulder a quick shake. "Don't make me grab the water tin."

"You wouldn't."

"Oh yes, I would." He smirked, returning to the fire.

"Ugh, I'm getting up."

Adeline pushed herself into a sitting position. A splitting headache thumped in her temples as she stared into the fire. The excessive heat or lack of sleep must've caused it. She rubbed her tired eyes, wishing she were anywhere but there.

"How'd you sleep?" Jesse asked, keeping his eyes on the small kettle heating over the flames.

"Not good," she mumbled, yawning into her hand. "The coyotes kept me up."

"Say no more." Jesse lifted the kettle using the hem of his shirt. "I've got exactly what you need."

He poured the steaming liquid into two tin mugs. A bitter, unmistakable aroma hit Adeline like a punch. She wrinkled her nose. She hated coffee.

"Here you go." Jesse offered her a mug.

Adeline made a face. "You know I don't like coffee."

"I promise you'll like it," Jesse said, inching the mug closer. "I loaded it with sweetener."

"All right. I'll try it."

The mug warmed her palms as she raised it to her mouth. It smelled surprisingly good, like chocolate and caramel blended into one. She gave it a quick blow before taking the tiniest sip. Sweetness burst across her tongue; she had barely swallowed before taking another sip.

Closing her eyes, she savored the rich flavor. It was like drinking a melted chocolate bar. "I didn't know coffee could taste this good."

"I told you," he said, handing her a hunk of bread.

Adeline bit into the baguette. It was soft and fresh, like it had just come out of the oven instead of Jesse's backpack.

The sun was high in the cloudless sky by the time they watered the horses and packed up camp. There wasn't a hint of humidity, but the heat was relentless. Sweat rolled down Adeline's back as she clipped her sleeping bag to the saddle and mounted Angela. Another grueling day was ahead.

They rode side by side through the dry terrain, baking beneath the harsh sun. For hours, they headed north, weaving through a maze of boulders and thick cactuses. They saw little to no wildlife, aside from a few lizards and snakes. Carcasses were far more common.

Sweating bullets, Adeline took a swig from her water tin. "It's so hot."

"There's a watering hole not too far from here," Jesse said, swiping his forehead with a dusty sleeve.

"How far?"

"Maybe a mile."

Adeline poured some water over her head. Lukewarm droplets rolled over her skin as she recapped the tin and shifted atop Angela. She was more than ready for a break.

They hadn't gone far when a cluster of rocks came into view. As they rounded the bend, a sparkling pool appeared, framed by palm trees and rugged stones. Lush green shrubs crowded the edges. It looked too tropical to be in the middle of a desert.

The first glimpse of water made the horses pick up speed. They stormed to the edge of the spring, dunking their heads into the clear water. Angela nearly threw Adeline off.

Adeline eased off Angela's back, her sneakers hitting the ground with a soft thud. Jesse followed suit, quickly unbuckling Regal's saddle and freeing him from the heavy load. He did the same for Angela, and the two horses plunged into the pool, lapping at the water as they swam.

Without hesitation, Jesse jumped in right behind them, not even bothering to remove his shirt. The soaked fabric clung to his skin as he stood, scrubbing the grime from his face and beard.

Not wanting to get fully wet, Adeline stayed at the water's edge. She submerged her arms in the pool and rubbed the red dust from her skin. It instantly cooled her down.

Water soaked her tank top as she splashed her face. It ran freely down her skin as she walked into the shade and redid her messy bun. A break from the sun felt good.

"We need to leave soon." Jesse walked out of the spring, squeezing the water from his shirt.

"Okay."

A light breeze drifted through the oasis, gently weaving through the brush and palm trees. Something bright flashed beside Adeline.

What's that?

She glanced down at the prickly weeds near her shoes but found nothing unusual.

Another glimmer of light sparkled within the brush. She had to investigate.

Dropping to her knees, Adeline parted the tall, coarse weeds. Dry stalks scraped her arms as she pried them open, revealing only rocks and dirt. But when she pushed aside another brittle shrub, she gasped.

A golden object gleamed up at her.

She reached into the brush, her heart pattering. The weeds scratched her skin as she plucked a golden pocket watch from the sandy ground.

Wiping away the dust, Adeline held it to the sun. It looked old. A cursive *W* was engraved on the casing, along with a few tiny scratches. Overall, it was in good shape.

She opened the timepiece with eager fingers. Though the interior had a few scuffs and the clock hands no longer moved, the watch was well-preserved.

Why would there be a pocket watch here?

She'd never seen a clock in that realm.

Adeline raced to Jesse, who was lounging beneath a palm tree.

"Look what I found!" she said, dropping beside him and shoving the pocket watch into his face.

Jesse chuckled, taking it from her hand. "You're always finding something."

"Why would a watch be out here?"

Jesse turned the old trinket over in his palm. "Looks like someone from your world brought it here and lost it."

"How come I've never met anyone from my world here?"

Jesse handed the watch back to her. "The few people who've made it here are either dead or living in a territory you've never been to."

"But how did they get here?"

"The same way you did."

The old, rusty fence in her backyard came to mind as she tucked the watch into her pocket. She still knew nothing about the only living Wilder who owned it and the woods it enclosed. She'd always assumed whoever it was had moved on from Black Mountain and had no clue what was beyond the chain-link barrier.

"Will I ever meet anyone from my world?" she asked.

"Yep."

"Really?" Her eyes grew big. "When?"

"You'll just have to wait and see." Jesse tapped her knee before rising. "Come on. It's time to go."

Jesse whistled for the horses while Adeline stood and wiped the dust from her jeans. Her mind buzzed with questions. Who would she meet? Would they be her age? What if it was someone she already knew?

Adeline smiled at the thought. Whoever it was, she hoped they'd cross paths soon.

Chapter Eight

The remainder of the day went by in a blur as Adeline and Jesse pressed onward. Desert vultures screeched above as the horses' hooves drummed against the rocky ground. They hadn't encountered any more predators, but Adeline was still on edge. There were plenty of hiding places in the desert.

"What exactly are we going to do once we get to Blistering Heights?" Adeline asked, bouncing slightly in the saddle.

"Join forces with the people there and take out the warriors who keep tormenting them," Jesse said.

Her gut churned. "You make it sound so simple."

"I'm not afraid of Ralock or his army," he said, his eyes focused ahead. "You shouldn't be either."

The horses stopped dead in their tracks. Adeline was thrown forward but stayed seated as a cloud of dust kicked up around them. "What's going on?"

"Hush," Jesse said.

Vultures circled above them as the light breeze created tornado-like funnels along the parched land. Heat waves rippled across the wasteland, warping the jagged rocks in the distance. Sweat stung Adeline's eyes, and she blinked hard to clear them. A sudden chill crept over her as the birds whined. Death was in the air; she could feel it in her bones.

"Get your bow." Jesse's voice penetrated her thoughts.

Hands trembling, Adeline grabbed her recurve bow and reached over her shoulder for an arrow. She quickly loaded it while scanning the wavering horizon.

At first, she saw nothing, only the distorted mirage of stone and sand, but then the blurry air began to shift. Figures formed inside the heat shimmer, their outlines rippling like water. Slowly, a pack of red wolves emerged from behind the rocks, growling and baring their teeth. Their fur was matted with dry blood and feces.

The foul stench of rotten eggs and decay almost made her gag.

Adeline's hair stood on end as she did a quick headcount. There were twenty-plus red wolves, with many showing signs of injury. Over half had defects—missing limbs, infected wounds—yet their mangled bodies did nothing to dull their aggression.

"Aim for the head," Jesse said, his muscles flexing as he raised his bow.

Adeline drew back her bowstring and locked onto the healthiest wolf leading the pack. She exhaled and released. The arrow slammed into the wolf's forehead, throwing it to the ground.

Chaos erupted. High-pitched howls split the air as the rest of the pack charged.

"Shoot 'em!" Jesse shouted, firing an arrow straight into a wolf's eye.

Angela and Regal stood firm while Adeline and Jesse picked off the wolves one by one. Wounded wolves dropped, yelping and twitching, as the remaining pack surged forward, leaving them behind. Their eyes burned with rage.

As the pack got closer, Jesse jumped off Regal.

"Get off Angela and use your dagger!" Jesse yelled, releasing another arrow.

Adeline dropped from the saddle, her feet stinging as they hit the hard ground. She flung aside her bow, drew her dagger, and faced the oncoming wolves. Her chest rose and fell in quick, panicked breaths.

Jesse was suddenly at her side, bow still in hand, as the horses charged. Regal and Angela barreled into the pack, trampling those too slow to dodge. The rest circled and snapped at their legs, but the horses fought back—biting, bucking, and stomping like warriors themselves.

"Let's go!" Jesse said, sprinting toward the fighting.

Adeline bolted after him, her hasty breaths matching the rush of adrenaline. She'd fought wolves in the combat simulator. This would be no different.

A sharp cry ripped from Angela as a wolf latched onto her hind leg. She wrenched free with a violent kick, just as Adeline stormed in. Adeline struck fast, slicing deep into the wolf's side. It howled, then went silent as her dagger plunged into its heart.

Blood splattered all over her as she yanked out her weapon from the wolf's chest. She barely turned before a wolf slammed into her from behind, knocking her face-first into the dirt. Dust filled her mouth as pain exploded in her shoulder.

Adeline screamed, twisting and bucking until the wolf tore free. Blood streamed down her arm as she scrambled to her feet. Before she could strike, Angela charged in. With a vicious kick, she smashed the wolf's face. Its head snapped back as it flew into a boulder with a sickening thud. When it didn't move, Angela spun and charged another wolf.

Adeline ignored the burn in her shoulder as a three-legged wolf lunged. She twisted clear of its snapping fangs and drove her dagger into its chest. Barking blared in her ears as another wolf leaped at her. She swung her dagger and sliced it in the mouth, nearly cutting off its entire jaw. Blood gushed onto the dry ground as the wolf retreated, whimpering loudly as it ran away.

It didn't get far. An arrow struck the back of its skull.

Adeline threw Jesse a quick look.

Standing on a rock, Jesse gave her a wink before facing the advancing dogs. There wasn't an ounce of fear on him as he tossed his bow into a nearby shrub and withdrew his longsword from his hip. He launched off the ledge, his sword severing the head of the nearest wolf. The other wolves lunged at him, but he easily slipped through their attacks as he danced through the desert. He hurtled over rocks and tore through any wolf that got too close.

How does he do that? Adeline wondered, glancing at the horses as they thundered after a few wolves trying to flee.

A sudden noise came from behind her.

Adeline whipped around, her dagger raised.

The blinding sun burned her eyes as a tall figure emerged from behind a boulder. She squinted, her pulse pounding.

It was a teenage boy.

Even from a distance, something about him was wrong. He stood utterly still, the desert wind tugging at his ragged clothes. He was as thin as a rail and filthy. Tattered fabric hung from his bony body, and a mess of dirty-blond dreadlocks dangled past his shoulders. His malnutrition and lack of hygiene made it hard to tell how old he was. He looked to be her age, maybe a little older.

Adeline blinked, half-expecting him to vanish like a mirage. The wavering heat made his outline ripple, warping his thin frame into something ghostlike.

But he was still there.

And he looked angry.

He stalked toward her, his expression sharper than the black dagger in his hand.

Adeline's heart thumped wildly. She was seeing a *real* person with a *real* weapon.

She took a step back, frantically searching for Jesse. The wolves were still attacking him, making him easy to spot. He was within earshot but too consumed by the fight to notice her distress.

She was on her own.

Fear surged through Adeline as she turned back to the furious boy.

The look in his eyes showed he was just as violent as the red wolves. Her instincts told her to fight, but she couldn't bring herself to take a human life. Maybe she could scare him off.

Adeline kept her dagger aimed at him. "Get back!"

The teenager ignored her, his pace quickening.

"I don't want to hurt you," she said, her voice edged with desperation.

He kept moving, closing the gap between them. Adeline had no choice but to fight.

The stranger slashed the black dagger through the air, missing her by inches as she sprang back. He snarled and swung again, this time at her chest. She easily avoided his amateur swing.

Having been trained by Jesse, Adeline could tell he had no real training with his weapon. His stance was sloppy, and his attacks were fast but clumsy. He'd wear himself out before he could do any real damage.

"I'm going to kill you!" he screamed, spit flying from his mouth.

Adeline flinched. His voice didn't sound human. Something was clearly wrong with him.

Before she could blink, the boy swung at her face. She jerked back but wasn't quick enough. A sharp sting seared her cheek, and she reached up to touch it. Her fingers came away red. The tip of his knife had grazed her cheek. It was a minor cut, but it was enough to make her mad.

"You're so dead," she growled, lunging forward. Her dagger slashed across his stomach, carving a clean line above his navel.

The boy screamed, stumbling back as blood speckled his torn shirt. He bared his yellow teeth and sent her a vile look. "That's the best you got?"

"I'm just getting started."

Adeline drove her dagger forward. The glass blade cut through the air, heading straight for his exposed neck. There was no avoiding it.

But the boy reacted quickly. His black dagger shot up just in time.

Sparks burst as the blades connected. The impact jolted Adeline's arm, flaring pain through her injured shoulder.

Her jaw tightened as she swung again, only to be blocked. More sparks flew.

He was a better fighter than she'd first assumed.

Determined to end the fight, Adeline drew back her arm and let out a fierce cry as she swung with all her might.

The weapons collided, and black shards exploded like a bomb. Adeline shielded her face in the crook of her arm. Slivers of glass pierced her forearm, sending fiery jolts of pain up her limb.

She lowered her arm. Dark specks littered the sunbaked ground; her dagger had obliterated his weapon.

Breathing heavily, Adeline plucked the glass shards from her skin and dropped them on the cracked terrain as she searched for the boy. He'd been thrown back several feet and was gasping for air on the ground. The hard impact must've knocked the wind out of him.

Adeline stomped toward him, dust kicking up around her sneakers. She was going to end his miserable life. He was still on his back, fighting for air, as Adeline loomed over him. Her hands shook with adrenaline as she raised her dagger above his scrawny chest.

"*No!*" Jesse shouted, his voice ripping through Adeline.

Adeline jumped and spun around. Jesse never used that tone unless it was serious.

Fury burned on his face as he stepped over the dead wolves, closing in fast. "Back up, Addie."

"He tried to kill me!" Adeline snapped, pointing her dagger at the boy.

"Put your weapon away *now*."

Adeline stepped away, blinking fast against the sudden tears. Her mind scrambled. Why was Jesse mad at her? She'd only been defending herself, using the very skills he'd taught her.

Swallowing the lump in her throat, Adeline sheathed her dagger, her body still shaking. There was no calming her racing heart as Jesse approached the filthy teenager.

"Hello, Caleb," Jesse said calmly, offering him a hand.

Adeline gasped and fell back a step. *Caleb?*

Disgust twisted across the teen's face as he slapped Jesse's hand away and pushed to his feet. He was a couple of inches shorter, but that didn't stop him from getting in Jesse's face.

"Screw you, Jesse." Caleb shoved him in the chest.

Jesse stumbled but kept his footing.

Adeline's mouth parted. *What is happening? How do they know each other?*

She clenched her fists, waiting for Jesse to retaliate. To teach Caleb a lesson. To do something.

But Jesse didn't react. He stayed calm and gave Caleb a compassionate look.

Before he could speak, Caleb spat in his face.

Adeline reeled back, anger rising again. If Jesse wouldn't defend himself, she would.

With a growl of outrage, she lunged. Her palms slammed into Caleb's chest, sending him crashing to the ground with a grunt. Adeline stood over him, her eyes blazing. "You better stay down."

A strong hand clamped onto Adeline's arm and yanked her back. It was Jesse, and he was angry. His grip bit into her bicep as he dragged her several paces away before letting go.

"You need to chill out," he said, each word low but sharp. "I'll handle this."

"He spit in your face!" Adeline motioned toward Caleb, who was already on his feet.

"I'm aware of that." Jesse's emerald eyes flashed as they locked with hers. "Now stay here."

Biting back a scream, Adeline fumed as he walked away. Sweat streaked down his back, darkening the fabric as he strode toward Caleb, the wind whipping sand around his boots. It took everything she had not to go after him.

Caleb lifted a piece of his destroyed blade, then, with a cry, hurled it at a rock. He tensed as Jesse approached. "Leave me alone."

"I know you're upset," Jesse said, raising his hands, "but you need to come with us."

Come with us? Adeline's breath caught. She must've misheard him. Surely Jesse wouldn't want that monster to tag along.

"This place isn't safe," Jesse said. "If you want to survive, you'll need our help."

Caleb straightened to his full height, his hatred evident. "I will *never* go anywhere with you again."

Turning on his heels, Caleb hobbled away. Dust rose in little clouds under his dragging steps, and he never looked back as he scrambled over a pile of rocks and vanished from sight.

Jesse lowered his head, wiping sweat and blood from his brow.

Adeline stormed up to him. "Why on earth would you want that psycho to come with us?"

Jesse looked at her, sadness clear in his gaze.

"Why are you upset, Jesse?" she demanded. "He nearly killed me!"

"He's deceived, Addie," Jesse said quietly, his eyes fixed on the spot where Caleb had gone. "He won't last long out here."

Adeline could tell Jesse truly cared about the dangerous guy named Caleb. But why? He was clearly nothing but trouble. "How do you know him?"

Jesse let out a sigh. "It's a long story."

"Do you mind sharing it?"

"Later." He gave her shoulder a quick pat as he walked by her.

She trailed after him. "Why can't you tell me now?"

Jesse stopped and faced her. "Addie, I know you have a lot of questions about Caleb. But now's not the time to answer them."

Blowing out a frustrated breath, Adeline watched Jesse retrieve his bow. He moved around the dead wolves and the desert vultures already picking at their remains. It was a gruesome sight. The desert looked like a battlefield, blood painting the rocks and soaking into the dry earth.

Angela trotted to Adeline, alert and ready. Blood speckled her white coat, and Adeline's heart dropped. "Are you hurt?"

Angela shook her head with a loud snort while Adeline inspected the bloodstains. There were a few scratches and bite marks on the mare's legs and belly, but most of the blood wasn't hers.

"You were so brave." Adeline scratched Angela's chin, wincing as pain spiked in her shoulder. She'd forgotten about the wolf bite. The blood and dirt made the teeth marks difficult to see. It throbbed as she pulled a water tin from her backpack and poured it over the wound.

The water stung as it washed away some of the grime. But not enough.

"Let me help." Jesse walked her way, the sun highlighting the blood splotches on his T-shirt and cargo pants.

He took the tin and tilted it until the water spilled over the wound. The pain was sudden, like a bee sting, but Adeline held perfectly still as Jesse examined the injury. Something clouded his features in a way she'd never seen before.

"Are you mad at me?" she asked.

"No." His eyes flicked to hers, just for a moment. "Are you mad at me?"

"I was when you yelled at me," she admitted, focusing on her arm, "but I'm not anymore."

"You would've killed Caleb if I hadn't stepped in."

"Why do you care about him?"

"I know what he has been through."

Caleb's grungy appearance came to Adeline's mind. It was obvious he was in bad shape. But why was he alone in the desert?

"Does he live out here?" she asked.

"No. He was traveling with those wolves."

That didn't surprise her. He was just as filthy and wild as they were. "Why?"

"So many questions." Jesse smiled, but it didn't reach his eyes as he assessed her shoulder.

"I'm just curious."

"I know you are. It's not every day you run into a teenager in the middle of nowhere."

Jesse poured more water on her shoulder, and another round of pain zapped down her arm. Adeline frowned as she looked at the bite. It was deep.

"That wolf really got you." Jesse set the water tin aside. "Good thing you've got a dagger that can seal it."

Adeline freed the shimmering glass blade from her hip, lifting it into the sunlight. Tiny rainbows swirled across the desert floor like light through a diamond. The dagger wasn't just powerful in battle; it had the rare ability to heal minor wounds. She'd lost count of how many times she'd relied on it in the past year, especially after tough training sessions in the combat simulator.

Adeline handed it to Jesse, and he pressed the blade to the bite. It burned at first, but the pain quickly faded. Her skin was sealed and back to normal.

"Good as new." Jesse ran his finger over the healed skin.

"Thanks," Adeline said, rolling her shoulder. "Feels way better."

"Good." Jesse tucked the dagger back in her sheath. "Let's get your bow and start moving. It'll be dark soon."

The heat pressed down on Adeline as she made her way back to where she'd tossed her recurve bow, with Angela a few steps behind her. Billows of dust formed with every step as she kept a cautious eye out for Caleb. He no longer had a weapon, but that didn't ease her suspicion. Was he watching her, calculating his next attack? That thought made her skin crawl.

She grabbed her bow, brushing off the dust, and muttered under her breath, "Hope I never see him again."

Chapter Nine

The mysterious boy named Caleb was still on Adeline's mind as she sat around the campfire with Jesse that night. It had been another excruciating day. She was glad it was coming to an end.

Rubbing her tired eyes, Adeline glanced at Jesse. He looked just as drained. He watched the fire in silence, his countenance somber. They hadn't spoken much since they'd set up camp. Was he thinking about Caleb too?

"You fought well today," Jesse said, shifting his eyes to her. "I'm proud of you."

"Thanks. You did too."

"Well, thank you." Jesse offered a faint grin as he leaned back against a rock.

The campfire danced and crackled, throwing spooky shadows along the boulders. Caleb crept back into Adeline's thoughts. Where was he now? Had he followed them? Was he still alive? He'd looked close to death; it wouldn't surprise her if he hadn't made it.

A deafening scream launched Adeline upright. She drew her dagger, mute with terror as goosebumps pebbled her arms. The night air suddenly felt colder.

Another scream split the dark. It was close. Really close.

"Stay here." Jesse darted into the darkness.

Panic squeezed her lungs as Adeline backed herself between both horses, their bodies warm and muscles tight beneath their calm stance. She felt safer with them close.

The ear-piercing cries continued. She couldn't tell if they belonged to an animal or a person, but whatever it was...it was in pain.

Did you find what's making that noise? Adeline asked Jesse in her mind.

No response.

The cries stopped.

Silence returned. All that could be heard was the crackling of the fire and her own ragged breathing.

Snap!

Adeline jolted, air catching in her throat.

Crack!

Heavy footsteps pounded nearby, advancing at a quick rate.

"Jesse?" she whispered, her voice shaky. "Is that you?"

Branches snapped as Jesse burst through the trees, carrying a lanky body in his arms. He neared the fire, the flames casting light across the figure.

Adeline gasped.

It was Caleb.

Limp in Jesse's arms, Caleb mumbled incoherently, like he'd been drugged. His right foot was a bloody mess. Blood soaked his tattered sneaker, making it hard to see the actual injury.

"I need water, bandages, and the medicine tin," Jesse said urgently, lowering Caleb beside the fire.

Adeline scrambled to his backpack. "Where's the medicine?"

"Front pocket."

Caleb groaned as Jesse carefully removed the ruined shoe while Adeline rummaged through Jesse's bag. She quickly found the supplies and rushed to his side.

A sickening stench wafted from Caleb, making Adeline take a step back. He smelled as though he hadn't bathed in months. But it wasn't the smell that turned her stomach. It was his foot.

Puncture wounds the size of quarters wrapped around his entire ankle, oozing blood like a faucet. It was worse than she'd imagined.

"He stepped into a bear trap." Jesse poured water over the mangled limb.

A whimper escaped Caleb as he bit down on his blistered lip. He twitched and moaned as Jesse gently smeared ointment on each wound. The strong smell of eucalyptus hung in the air as Adeline observed silently. Despite herself, compassion began to grow within her. It wasn't much, but enough to make her want to help.

"Do you want to use my dagger to heal his wounds?" Adeline asked, hovering over Jesse's shoulder.

"No." Jesse didn't look up as he kept rubbing the paste on Caleb's swollen ankle.

"Why not?"

"He's not ready for that," Jesse said flatly.

Not ready? Her brow furrowed as she looked at Caleb's shredded foot. The dagger could fix it in seconds. Why wouldn't Jesse want that?

Adeline stood in silent confusion behind Jesse as he worked. Caleb was no longer whining or moving. He looked dead; his filthy dreadlocks fanned around his head like a halo. Only the faint rise and fall of his skinny chest confirmed he was still alive.

The firelight flickered against his face as he slept, giving Adeline her first real look at him. He looked different now that he wasn't trying to kill her. The harsh anger had faded from his expression, leaving behind an unexpected softness in his features.

With defined cheekbones and a symmetrical face, he could be quite handsome if he were properly nourished. But he'd need to chop off the dreadlocks and bathe for hours. A trip to the dentist wouldn't hurt either. He clearly hadn't seen a toothbrush in a while.

The longer she stared, the more she saw his potential. What had he looked like before? And what would he look like after he got cleaned up?

Adeline's imagination screeched to a halt when Jesse shot her a grin.

Heat rushed to her cheeks as she averted her eyes and quickly moved to the opposite side of the fire. Her muscles tensed as she sat down, silently kicking herself for being so curious. She kept forgetting Jesse could hear her thoughts like they were his own.

Her face continued to burn as Jesse finished wrapping Caleb's ankle and tucked the supplies back into his pack. She focused on the flames, refusing to meet Jesse's eyes when he settled next to her.

"So," he said. "You think he's attractive?"

"I never said that."

"But you thought it." Jesse nudged her with his shoulder.

"You're being ridiculous."

"Don't worry." Jesse bit back a smile. "I won't tell him."

Adeline shot him an irritated look, which only deepened his amusement. He was clearly teasing her. She knew that, but it didn't make her any less embarrassed.

"He wouldn't have made it through the night if I'd left him out there," Jesse said, eyeing Caleb with concern.

"What did he do when he saw you?" Adeline asked, tossing a stick into the flames.

"He asked for my help."

She huffed. "That's surprising."

"People have a change of heart when they're desperate."

"What are we going to do with him?" Adeline asked. "He can't walk."

"I have a plan."

Adeline waited, hoping he would elaborate. He didn't. "I'm guessing you're not going to tell me."

"Not yet."

She rolled her eyes. "Typical."

"I'm heading to bed." Jesse stood and stretched before heading to his sleeping bag near Caleb. "You should too."

Adeline didn't argue. She got ready for bed, her limbs heavy with exhaustion. Sliding into her sleeping bag, she pulled it up to her chin and shut her weary eyes. The grime clinging to her skin itched, but she was too preoccupied with Caleb to care.

She wanted to know more about him. Where was he from? How did he end up in the desert? Why did he look so terrible? How did he know Jesse? He clearly hated Jesse...but why?

The same questions plagued her mind as discomfort pulsed through her sore body. She longed for a real bed.

An owl hooted in the distance while the dying fire crackled beside her. With a final yawn, she drifted to sleep.

CHAPTER TEN

ADELINE TOSSED AND TURNED all night. Once she opened her eyes, there was no going back to sleep. The sky was a soft pink when she rose for the day. Everyone was asleep. Even the horses.

The desert was beginning to stir as Adeline tiptoed past Caleb. He was in the same spot as before, soft snores pouring from his open mouth. He looked peaceful and innocent like he hadn't tried to kill her the day before.

Adeline shook her head; she knew better than to believe that.

Her sneakers crunched against the stony ground as she slipped away. She didn't go far. The sunrise painted the sky in glorious colors as she sat on a rock that overlooked the quiet desert. It was extraordinary, almost enough to make her forget how much she hated that area. Almost.

Adeline adjusted her leg into a more comfortable position. Something jostled in her pocket.

The pocket watch.

She'd forgotten all about it.

Adeline pulled out the gold timepiece and turned it over in her hand. The engraved *W* on the casing glinted in the sunlight. If only it could somehow tell her about its owner.

"You're up early," a voice said from behind her.

Adeline leaped to her feet and spun around, only to find Jesse standing there.

"It's just me," he said with a soft chuckle.

Adeline sat back down, her heart fluttering. "You scared me."

Jesse settled beside her, dragging a hand down his tired face. He was a mess. His clothes and sun-kissed skin were streaked with blood and grime, and his hair had come loose from its bun.

"How far is Blistering Heights from here?" Adeline asked, sliding the watch back into her pocket.

"Not far." Jesse kept his eyes on the sunrise.

Adeline followed his stare. Soft pinks mingled with faint golds along the horizon, their glow spilling slowly across the rocky desert. The peaceful view begged her to relax, but even in the soft light, unease lingered at the back of her mind. One thought kept tugging at her...Caleb.

"What do you want to do with Caleb?" she asked.

Silence stretched between them. Jesse didn't answer right away, his focus lingering on the glowing sky. After a long pause, he turned to her. "Addie, I've got a favor to ask."

A knot formed in her throat. Jesse never asked for favors. "Okay."

"You're not going to like it."

"What is it?"

He scratched his thick beard. "I need you to take Caleb to the cabin...while I go to Blistering Heights."

"*What?*" Adeline shot up. "You can't be serious."

"He needs our help," Jesse said evenly as he rose to stand with her.

"Absolutely not," she said, parking her hands on her hips. "He tried to murder me yesterday."

"He will die if we don't help him."

"I don't care!"

"Well, I do," Jesse said, his jaw tight and stare firm.

Adeline grumbled as she looked back at the sunrise. She wouldn't travel with Caleb. Not by herself. There had to be another way. "Why can't we just take him to Blistering Heights, and then we all go back to your cabin together?"

"He won't survive the trip."

"We could protect him."

"Addie." Jesse placed his calloused hands on her shoulders. "Please. Do this for me."

Adeline shrugged off his hands and started to pace. Her blood boiled as she kicked a tumbleweed like a soccer ball, sending it rolling across the rocks. She spun back toward him. "What if he attacks me again?"

"He won't."

"He did yesterday!"

Jesse stuffed his hands into his pockets, his expression softening. "I need your help, Addie."

Guilt struck her as she searched his emerald eyes. He'd done so much for her. What had she ever done for him?

"I can't believe I'm saying this." Adeline kneaded her forehead. "But fine. I'll take that crazy boy to the cabin."

Jesse clapped his hands together with a proud grin. "I knew I could count on you."

"Just so you know," she added, "if he attacks me, I *will* fight back."

"I don't doubt it."

Adeline scanned the infinite desert, anxiety starting to build. There were some natural landmarks, but most everything looked the same. It would be so easy to get lost.

"How am I supposed to find the cabin?" she asked. "I don't know this area."

"The horses know the way."

"Regal's not going with you?" she asked, her stomach knotting.

Jesse shook his head. "He's going with you."

"What about you?"

"I'll walk. It's not far."

A pang of concern surged through Adeline, but it quickly turned to relief. At least she wouldn't have to ride double with Caleb. That would've only made things worse.

"Let's head back to camp," Jesse said, starting down the path. "You two need to leave as soon as possible."

"What's the rush?" Adeline fell into step beside him.

"He's not safe here. They'll come looking for him soon."

"Who will?"

Jesse didn't respond.

He probably attacked someone, Adeline thought to herself. *Or stole something.*

The smell of campfire still lingered as they entered camp. Adeline slowed to a stop when she caught Caleb's nasty glare. Hatred burned in his eyes. He wanted to hit her; she was sure of it.

Jesse didn't flinch at Caleb's harsh demeanor as he knelt beside him and pulled a loaf of bread from his backpack. He offered it to Caleb. "I bet you're hungry."

Caleb snatched the food and tore into it with his teeth. Adeline stared. Had he been raised by animals?

"Let me check your foot," Jesse said, pulling supplies from his bag.

The hardness returned to Caleb's face, but he said nothing as he devoured the rest of the bread.

For the next few minutes, Jesse doctored Caleb's ankle. He discarded the blood-soaked bandage and reapplied the ointment before wrapping it again. Caleb squirmed and gritted his teeth the entire time, but he never pulled away.

"Your wounds are healing." Jesse stood, wiping his hands on his pants. "But you won't be able to walk for a while."

Caleb glared up at Jesse, his nostrils flaring.

"This is Adeline Bigsby." Jesse nodded toward her. "She's going to take you to my cabin."

Caleb didn't even glance at her. His glare stayed locked on Jesse, his lips curling in disgust. "I'm not going there."

"You don't have much of a choice right now, do you?" Jesse placed his hands on his hips.

"I'd rather die than go there."

"Suit yourself," Jesse said, shrugging as he started packing up camp. He motioned for Adeline to do the same. She held back a comment, her fingers digging into the sleeping bag as she rolled it tight. Her jaw ached from clenching, but she kept her irritation hidden.

"You can't just leave me here!" Caleb screamed.

"Yes, I can," Jesse said coolly, fastening his pack. "You can either go with Adeline or stay here alone."

Caleb pounded his fists into the rocky ground, screaming at the top of his lungs. It didn't faze Jesse. He ignored him and kept packing. So did Adeline.

Why does he want to help this crazy person? Adeline bit off a piece of beef jerky before packing it away. *He clearly doesn't want our help.*

Caleb kept screaming like his life depended on it. His face grew red, but he didn't stop. On and on, his yells persisted.

Finally, he wore himself out. Gasping for air, he rubbed his raw, dust-covered knuckles.

"What'll it be, Caleb?" Jesse asked, squatting to meet his eyes. "Are you going with Adeline or staying here?"

"I'll go with her," he muttered through clenched teeth.

"What was that?"

"I said, I'll go with her!"

"Great." Jesse rose and went to Regal. Grabbing the reins, he guided the massive horse over to Caleb.

Caleb's eyes widened as he craned his neck to take in Regal's towering form. Jesse hoisted Caleb like a toddler, placing his good foot in the stirrup. Caleb swung his injured leg over, shaking as he clutched the reins. He was obviously afraid, but the way he settled into the saddle told Adeline he'd ridden before.

"I'm sure you remember Regal," Jesse said, patting the stallion's side. "In case you've forgotten, he doesn't like to be messed with. He also really likes Adeline, so I suggest you behave."

Caleb went pale, terror flashing across his face.

Jesse gave Adeline a wink as he slung his backpack over his shoulder and grabbed his bow. He walked over to her and guided her away from Caleb and Regal until they were out of view.

Teary-eyed, Adeline latched onto Jesse. He smelled of sweat and blood as she buried her face in his T-shirt. "Please don't make me do this."

Jesse wrapped her in a firm hug, his heartbeat steady against her ear. "You're going to be okay, Addie."

The tears continued to flow as she held on to Jesse. She didn't want to face the desert alone. Especially not with Caleb. But she'd made Jesse a promise, and she intended to keep it.

"Please be careful." Adeline pulled back and wiped her eyes. "I don't know what I'd do without you."

"Always." He gave her a gentle smile.

Adeline rubbed her cheeks once more before heading back to the horses with Jesse, forcing her expression into something neutral. She forced a steady breath through her nose; she didn't want Caleb to know she'd been crying.

Lifting her chin, Adeline trailed behind Jesse, doing her best to mask her rising fear. Pebbles crunched underfoot as she went to Angela and mounted, never once looking at Caleb.

"Stop for no one," Jesse said as he adjusted her stirrup. "You need to get out of here as fast as you can."

Adeline dipped her head once. "Okay."

"Be brave, Addie." Jesse gave her a quick, crooked grin. "I'll see you soon."

Adeline mustered a weak smile before nudging Angela forward. The journey had officially begun.

The sun climbed higher as Regal followed behind, Caleb silently rocking on his back. He looked like a child atop the huge beast.

A mix of fear and unease churned in Adeline's gut as they ventured into the open desert, its endless expanse making her feel small and exposed. She had to protect herself. Not just from wild animals, but from Caleb too. He could turn on her at any moment.

Her blood ran cold at the thought, but she shook it away. Now wasn't the time to dwell on it. They had a long journey ahead, and she needed to be alert and ready for anything.

Chapter Eleven

The horses raced ahead, kicking up dust as their hooves clapped against the rocky earth. Adeline was grateful for the breeze. Sweat rolled down her back, but it wasn't nearly as unbearable as the day before.

She had one thing on her mind—getting back to the cabin as fast as possible.

It had been hours since they had parted ways with Jesse, but the tight knot in her chest hadn't loosened. She stayed tense, scoping the area for any signs of danger. Thankfully, she hadn't seen anything other than a few lizards darting to safety.

The terrain turned rugged, forcing the horses to slow their pace. They moved in a single-file line through the boulders, Angela in the lead.

Tightening her grip on the reins, Adeline rocked with the horse's stride. Caleb hadn't spoken since they'd left camp, but she looked back in time to catch his glare. It was just as hideous as his appearance. His bloody shirt had more holes than fabric; so did his remaining shoe. She could see his blistered toes poking through the top.

"Just so you know, I'm not staying at the cabin," Caleb said, his dreadlocks swinging with each bounce of the saddle.

Adeline rolled her eyes and faced forward again. "I don't care what you do once we get there."

"I used to be naive like you," he said. "Thinking Jesse was a good guy; believing I could trust him."

Adeline's knuckles turned white as she fisted the reins. It took all her self-control to keep her mouth shut.

"It's only a matter of time before you see what he's really like," Caleb continued.

Adeline jerked the reins, bringing Angela to a stop. Dust curled around them as she pivoted in the saddle. "I don't know why you hate Jesse so much, but you're a pathetic fool who tricked *my friend* into helping you."

Caleb scoffed. "You call this helping me? He kidnapped me and forced me against my will."

"Kidnapped? Really?" Adeline shook her head in disbelief. "Jesse rescued you from a bear trap, patched up your foot, and sent you with me."

"I didn't want to come with you!"

"That makes two of us!"

Caleb's eyes went cold and ugly. "I'm going to make your life hell."

"You already have," she said, sounding as angry as she felt. "Now shut up."

Adeline was shaking as she got Angela moving again. *I hate him so much.*

The temptation to leave Caleb stranded in the desert was strong. It got stronger the longer she meditated on it. It would be so easy to pull him off Regal and leave him behind. No one would miss him.

"Be kind to him."

Jesse's voice startled Adeline as she rode atop Angela. She wasn't expecting to hear from him so soon. A pang of guilt made her put a stop to such thoughts. Being kind to someone like Caleb felt impossible, but she would try for Jesse's sake.

The hours dragged on, and the relentless heat didn't let up. It pounded against them as they trotted forward. Adeline raised a hand to the bright sun. They must've missed the watering hole Jesse had taken her to the day before. It was nowhere in sight.

Sighing, she wiped the sweat from her brow before grabbing her water tin. She took a long swig, then another. The water wasn't cold, but it soothed her dry throat.

Adeline glanced back to check on Caleb. His head hung low as he bounced in the saddle. He looked like he was about to fall off.

She ran a hand down her face. She hated the idea of sharing her water with him. But he wouldn't make it if she didn't.

Adeline slowed Angela until they were riding next to Regal. "Do you want some water?"

Caleb looked her way and nodded once.

"Don't put your lips on it." Adeline handed him the tin.

Caleb reached for it with a dirty hand, grime packed beneath each fingernail. Faded scars marked his arm. Some were small, others long and jagged. Adeline wondered where they'd come from.

He tipped the tin over his mouth, water rolling down his chin and neck as he drank. He didn't stop until it was empty. Without a word, he tossed it back to her.

Adeline caught it, expecting a thank you. It never came.

She tucked the tin away. "Is it that hard to say thank you?"

Caleb grunted something unintelligible as he wiped his mouth with the back of his hand.

She still had plenty of water in her backpack, thanks to Jesse, but that wasn't the point. Her lips settled into a firm line as she moved Angela ahead of Regal. She couldn't stand being near him.

As the sun began to sink, Adeline's anxiety grew. She needed to find a campsite before dark. Ideally, the same one they'd used the first night, but she wasn't sure where it was. Everything looked the same.

She leaned close to Angela's ear and whispered, "Do you know where we camped the first night?"

Angela snorted and nodded her head.

"Are we close?"

Another nod.

Relief flooded Adeline as she eased back in the saddle. Hopefully, they'd reach it before dark.

Ten minutes passed, and her heart jumped when the original campsite came into view.

Finally!

With a swift kick, Adeline sent Angela into a gallop, leaving Regal in a cloud of dust. The stallion let out an angry neigh and charged after them.

The wind whipped against Adeline's ears, but it wasn't loud enough to cover Caleb's screams. She looked back and had to bite her lip to keep from laughing. He clung to the saddle, bouncing violently, his eyes wide with panic.

Regal caught up to Angela, and they flew past rocks and desert shrubs. It wasn't long before they reached their destination. They skidded to a stop, nearly launching Caleb over Regal's head. He was panting so hard, Adeline worried he'd have a heart attack.

"You're fine, Caleb." Adeline dismounted Angela. "Just breathe."

"You...are...crazy." He drew a breath between each word.

"I've been called worse."

Adeline grinned to herself as she entered the hideout, the horses trailing behind her. It looked exactly as she'd left it. She gave the place a quick scan before unclipping her stuff from Angela's saddle.

"How am I supposed to get down?" Caleb asked, eyeing the ground like it was miles away.

Before she could answer, Regal lowered himself until his belly touched the dusty floor. Pain rippled across Caleb's face as he slid off, careful not to bump his injured foot. Once he was on solid ground, he scooted away from Regal.

"I'm going to get some wood," Adeline said and left Caleb there.

The sun was setting as Adeline scanned the area. She kept her hand on her dagger as she hustled toward a cluster of trees, her pulse hammering in her ears. Once she saw it was safe, she scooped up as many dry sticks as she could carry and hustled back to the hideout.

Caleb sat in the corner with his arms crossed, his eyes burning a hole through her. She ignored him as she dumped the sticks into the firepit and grabbed the matches from her backpack. After arranging the wood as best she could, she struck a match.

The flame went out the moment it touched the wood.

Ugh.

She tried again. Same thing.

Adeline scratched her forehead with a huff. Starting a fire was hard enough without Caleb watching her every move. She fired him a look. "What are you looking at?"

"You're doing it wrong."

"Oh, really? You think you can do it better?"

"I know I can." He scooted forward. "I was a Boy Scout."

Adeline's face scrunched. "A Boy Scout?"

Caleb stared at her, watching her reaction like he was gauging whether the name meant anything to her. She knew exactly what a Boy Scout was in her world. Was there something in that realm with the same name?

"Fine." Adeline tossed him the pack of matches. "You do it."

The matches landed beside Caleb, and he immediately went to work rearranging the pile of sticks. He placed the smallest twigs in a tight bundle, then stacked the longer ones in a teepee around it. It took only one match for the wood to ignite.

Caleb blew gently on the fire, and the flames blazed to life. It was so hot, Adeline had to take a step back.

"Not bad," Adeline said, forcing the words out as she returned to her backpack. She came back with a handful of food and sat near Caleb. There was still some distance between them, just in case he snapped.

Caleb kept his eyes on the food, drool pooling at the corner of his mouth.

"Here." Adeline tossed him a pack of beef jerky.

Caleb snatched the jerky in midair and ripped into it before Adeline had taken her first bite. He devoured the meat as if it were his last meal.

Adeline watched him in silence, chewing slowly. The more she studied him, the more she was convinced that he wasn't from her world. He acted more savage than human, and his appearance implied he lived in the desert.

But that couldn't be right.

Jesse had said Caleb didn't live there.

"Where are you from?" she asked.

Caleb sat up straight, coldness lacing his glare. "Give me more food, and I'll tell you."

Adeline released a frustrated breath. She didn't want to play his stupid game, but she wanted answers. With a reluctant sigh, she tossed him another pack of jerky. He consumed it in seconds. "Are you going to answer my question now?"

Caleb tossed the empty wrapper into the fire and watched it curl into ash. "I'm not from this world."

Adeline stiffened. "Where are you from, then?"

"I was born in a place called Black Mountain."

Shock rippled through Adeline, stealing the air from her lungs. Her thoughts scattered in every direction. Jesse told her she'd meet someone from her world. She never imagined it would be Caleb.

"That's where I live," she said, keeping her voice level.

A flicker of surprise crossed Caleb's face as he threw her a quick glance. He diverted his eyes back to the fire, confusion growing in his stare.

Adeline waited for him to say something. To ask her anything.

Nothing. Not even a smart-aleck remark.

Adeline exhaled slowly and looked his way again. He was deep in thought, clueless about her stares as he rubbed the back of his neck. There was something large and black on his forearm. It looked like dried blood.

"Did you hurt your arm?" Adeline asked.

He quickly tucked his arm away. "No."

"Whatever, dude," she said, holding up her hands. "I'm just trying to be nice."

"I don't need you to be nice to me," he growled.

"Clearly."

Adeline's face flushed, and it wasn't from the fire. She walked away, trying to rein in her rising temper. Maybe keeping herself busy would help distract her.

She unrolled her sleeping bag across the flames from Caleb and removed her quiver, rubbing the knot from her shoulder as she went to get Jesse's sleeping bag.

"Catch." She threw it at Caleb.

He didn't react quickly enough, and the sleeping bag hit him in the head.

"Watch it!" he snapped, his glare sharp enough to cut.

"Oops." A smirk pulled on Adeline's lips as she settled onto her bed. She slipped out of her dusty shoes and unbuckled her sheath, tucking the dagger deep inside her sleeping bag before climbing in. She couldn't risk Caleb grabbing it in the middle of the night.

Surely he wouldn't try to hurt her while she slept. Would he?

She shook the thought away. The horses would never allow it.

Tiredness pulled at her eyelids as she shifted, trying to get comfortable. It had been a long day, and she was ready for it to be over.

Listening to the quiet pops of the fire, Adeline looked up at the dark sky, her mind refusing to settle. It was running wild. Mostly about Caleb.

How did he get here? she wondered.

Nothing about him made sense. He looked and acted like a madman, yet he was from her world. And not only that. He was from Black Mountain.

What happened to him?

"Where did you get that dagger?" Caleb asked, breaking the silence.

"I found it."

"Where at?"

"None of your business." Adeline kept her eyes on the stars.

She felt Caleb's glare burning through her, though she didn't look his way. She smirked. It felt good to give him a taste of his own medicine.

Inhaling the cool night air, Adeline still couldn't believe she was stuck with Caleb. He wasn't just intolerable. He was helpless. If danger showed up, he wouldn't be able to do anything but hide. In her mind, he was useless, and she couldn't wait to get rid of him.

Her thoughts wandered to Jesse. Had he made it to Blistering Heights? Had he fought any warriors yet? Was he safe? She thought about talking to him through her thoughts but didn't want to distract him.

Rolling onto her side, Adeline winced. Her tender muscles desperately needed a break. She ached for a long, hot shower and her soft bed back at the cabin.

One more day, and I'll be done with this idiot.

She closed her eyes and let sleep take her.

Chapter Twelve

A blood-chilling scream ripped Adeline from her sleep. Her eyes snapped open, and she was on her feet in an instant, dagger in hand. The morning sun gave her enough light to see that the screams were coming from Caleb. He was thrashing around in his sleeping bag.

Something was attacking him!

Adeline rushed to his side, searching for the assailant as Caleb screamed his head off. Then reality hit her. He was sound asleep.

"Wake up!" Adeline shook him.

Caleb launched himself up, panting as he looked in all directions. "What happened? Where am I?"

Adeline rubbed her tired eyes, her heart racing as she tried to control her heavy breathing. "You must've had a nightmare."

Caleb didn't respond. His thin chest rose and fell rapidly as he stared straight ahead. Whatever he'd seen in his dream had terrified him.

Adeline grabbed one of the full water tins and held it out. "Drink this."

His hand trembled as he took it, still trying to catch his breath. When he lifted it to his lips, Adeline caught a glimpse of something on his forearm. It was the same arm he'd hidden from her the night before. Now, in the daylight, she saw it clearly.

It wasn't dry blood.

It was a tattoo.

A black cobra curled along his arm with its fangs out. It looked so lifelike, Adeline half-expected it to leap off his skin and strike her.

Tattoos had never bothered Adeline, but there was something strange about his. It gave her an eerie feeling that she couldn't shake.

"Nice tattoo," she said, tilting her chin toward his forearm.

Caleb pressed his arm tight against his chest, covering the tattoo.

"No offense, but I hate snakes."

"I do too," he said quietly.

"Then why'd you put one on your arm?"

Caleb brushed his dreadlocks off his bony shoulder and gazed into the firepit, keeping his arm hidden from view. A shadow passed over his face, and for a moment, he looked almost haunted. Adeline waited for a reply, but he just sat there in silence.

Of course he wasn't going to tell her.

Weirdo.

Adeline went straight to her bed and sheathed her dagger before buckling it around her waist. Slipping her feet into her sandy sneakers, she walked over to her backpack. She needed to check Caleb's ankle before she forgot.

Adeline fumbled through her bag. No medicine, but she did find a roll of elastic bandage. It would have to do.

"I need to check your ankle before we leave," she said, holding up the bandage.

"No."

Adeline exhaled as she rubbed her forehead. "We don't have time for this."

"I said no." Caleb whipped his head toward her. His golden-green eyes were striking, even captivating, but the fury behind them erased all beauty.

"Do you want it to get infected?" she asked, her tone laced with frustration.

Caleb muttered something to himself. A moment later, he shifted his dirty foot in her direction. He wouldn't look at her as she slowly unwound the soiled bandage.

A foul smell filled her nostrils, but she maintained her composure, tossing the bandage onto the embers. Dry blood crusted his ankle, but the puncture wounds beneath were healing fast. Far too fast. They looked more like old scars than fresh injuries.

Curious about their tenderness, Adeline gently touched one with her finger.

Caleb jerked his foot, almost kicking her in the face. "Don't touch it!"

"I'm trying to help you," Adeline said through clenched teeth.

"By reopening them?"

"Forget it." She slammed the roll of bandages into his hand. "You do it."

Adeline stormed off, grumbling to herself as she packed up camp. The faster they got to the cabin, the better.

I can't believe I'm helping this crazy boy! She rolled up her sleeping bag with extra force. *He deserves to rot out here.*

"Be kind to him," Godfrey said internally.

Adeline wasn't fazed by his voice slipping into her thoughts. It happened quite often. *"He doesn't deserve it."*

"There were times in your life when you didn't deserve it either."

Conviction hit Adeline as a strong memory emerged, one she would never forget. She could vividly recall screaming at Godfrey on the beach, her fists pounding into his chest. She had deserved his wrath, but all she got was his kindness. And that was what had ultimately healed her broken heart.

Sighing, Adeline undid her messy bun and massaged her aching scalp. She had no interest in being nice to Caleb. But she had to try.

"I'll try, Godfrey."

"That's my girl."

Adeline's lips lifted a little as she glanced over her shoulder. Caleb was still attempting to wrap his ankle. It wasn't going well. A string of curses spewed from his mouth as he unwrapped the bandage and tried again.

Why is he so angry?

There had to be a reason he acted that way.

Adeline tied her hair back up and continued packing. It didn't take her long to break down the campsite and get the horses ready for the day.

Once everything was done, she took a breath, pushed aside her lingering irritation, and approached Caleb. "I'm sorry I yelled at you."

Caleb didn't respond. He focused on his ankle, fumbling with the bandage.

"Let me wrap it for you."

"I don't need your help," Caleb snarled without looking up.

Adeline balled her fists, biting back the words she wanted to hurl. Her pulse thudded in her ears as she wrestled to stay calm.

Just as she searched for what to say next, something moved behind Caleb.

Squinting, Adeline locked onto the movement. Her heart dropped. It was a rattlesnake.

"Caleb," she whispered, "don't move."

Caleb shot her a glare, opened his mouth to speak, then fell silent at the unmistakable sound of a rattle. Slowly, he turned his head.

The snake was coiled, ready to strike.

His eyes went wide with fear.

Adeline snatched her bow from the saddle and nocked an arrow. "Sit still," she breathed, raising the bow.

"Please don't kill me," Caleb begged, desperation cracking through his voice.

Adeline's muscles ached as she pulled the bowstring tight, her fingers anchoring near her mouth. Her aim had to be perfect. Missing wasn't an option. Not this time.

She let go.

The arrow pinned the snake in place. It flipped and thrashed savagely as Caleb scrambled away. Adeline dropped the bow, drew her dagger, and sliced off the snake's head. It continued to twitch as she backed up and stowed her blade.

"I'm wrapping your ankle, and then we're leaving," she said, grabbing the compression wrap and dropping to her knees beside Caleb.

Caleb stared at the dead snake, his body trembling as Adeline wrapped his ankle. Again, she was struck by how quickly it was healing. She was certain he could walk, but she wasn't about to tell him that. The last thing she needed was for him to run away.

When she finished, she offered him a hand. He eyed it suspiciously before taking it.

Pulling him upright, she steadied him as he shifted his weight onto his good foot. As soon as he was balanced, she stepped back. Being close to him made her uncomfortable, plus he smelled like a pigpen.

Regal stepped between them and lowered himself. Caleb hesitated but eventually crawled onto Regal's back as Adeline prepared to leave. She double-checked the campsite before mounting Angela.

Without saying a word, she led the way, leaving nothing behind but the dead snake.

Chapter Thirteen

THE SUN BLAZED ABOVE as the horses moved at a quick speed, even faster than the day before. This portion of the desert was easier to navigate, and Adeline took full advantage of it. Getting to the cabin was all that mattered.

Time seemed to fly, and Adeline's heart took flight when she saw the steep hill that led to the forest. It was still off in the distance, but within reach.

Wanting to give the horses a little break, Adeline gently tugged on the reins until Angela slowed to a walk. Regal matched her speed, walking by her side. Adeline took the opportunity to check on Caleb, who'd been quiet the whole trip. He looked drained and weak as he swayed in the saddle, but he didn't seem as scared as before.

"Thanks for killing that snake," Caleb said, glancing in her direction.

"You're welcome." Adeline kept her face forward, masking her astonishment. She couldn't believe he had actually thanked her.

The next few minutes were silent aside from the thud of the horses' hooves and Adeline's wandering mind. Caleb and his life in Black Mountain occupied her thoughts.

Does he go to my school? she wondered. *Do we know the same people?*

She had no plans to be his friend, but perhaps she could learn more about him.

"How old are you?" Adeline asked.

Caleb shrugged. "I guess I'm still eighteen."

"You guess?"

"Time doesn't move when we're here," he said, wiping the beads of sweat from his forehead. "I was eighteen the last time I walked into the forest; I've been stuck here since."

Adeline furrowed her brows. "Stuck?"

"Yeah, I've been trapped in this realm for a long time," he said, a shadow darkening his features. "I stopped counting after the first year."

"Did you forget the way back?" she asked. "I can take you."

Caleb stared ahead, his frown deepening. "I know exactly how to get back to our world."

"Then why haven't you gone back?"

"My master has kept me here."

Adeline's skin crawled. "Your master?"

Caleb nodded slightly. "I ran away from him a few days ago; it won't be long before he comes after me."

It took Adeline a second to absorb the shock of his words. She'd never heard of such a thing in that realm. Then again, she knew very little about the other territories. Maybe slavery was acceptable in some areas.

"Why don't you just go back to Black Mountain now?" Adeline asked. "You'd be safe there."

"There's nothing left for me there," he said, his harsh demeanor returning. "It's better if I stay here and start over in a new territory."

"But what if your master finds you?"

"Then I'll be dead." His eyes flicked to hers, grim and sure, before drifting back to the desert.

Chills slithered down Adeline's back as she did a slow scan of the area. Who was his master? Was he searching for Caleb now? What if he caught up with them?

Adeline shivered at the thought. They had to get to the cabin; it was the only place they'd be safe.

A dry breeze whisked through the desert, lifting dust into the air as the horses reached the base of the steep hill. Adeline had to crane her neck to see the top. It looked steeper than before.

"Wait here," she told Caleb as she nudged Angela forward.

Angela started up the path, her hooves sinking into the loose sand. She made little progress before sliding back down to the bottom. With a burst of speed, she tried once more. Same results.

After several failed attempts, Adeline gave up. Climbing was out of the question for them.

Adeline scratched her sweaty scalp. *What do we do now?*

"There's another way." Henry's pleasant accent entered her mind.

Adeline sighed in relief. *"Where is it?"*

"It's hidden inside those evergreens."

Shading her eyes, Adeline surveyed the wall of sturdy trees about a football field away. Her stomach twisted as the thick green branches flaunted next to the red desert.

"We can't go in there," she said, trying not to panic. *"That leads to the Dark Territory."*

"Not all of it," Henry said. *"There's a secret path that will take you around Ralock's land and into the forest."*

Adeline fiddled with the reins while biting her bottom lip. *"Where's the path?"*

"Enter the evergreens and head west until you find a boulder shaped like a wolf's mouth," he said with certainty. *"That's where you will find the forgotten path."*

Adeline focused on the evergreens, anxiety rising in the back of her throat. Every part of her screamed to stay away, but what other option did they have?

"How are we supposed to get up that?" Caleb asked, raising a hand to the sun.

"We can't." Adeline steered Angela toward the evergreen forest. "We have to go this way."

Caleb went white. "I'm not going in there."

"Yes, you are."

"No, I'm not!"

Adeline pinched the bridge of her nose. "Why do you have to make everything so difficult?"

Caleb yanked his foot out of the stirrup and dropped the reins. "You can't make me."

"Calm down, Caleb," Adeline said, raising her voice. "You're going to hurt yourself."

Caleb tumbled off Regal, landing straight on his back. A puff of dust floated around him as he stared upward, his breath coming in ragged gasps.

Unbelievable! Adeline dismounted Angela and stomped up to Caleb.

"What's wrong with you?" Adeline asked, throwing her hands in the air.

Caleb rocked his head back and forth, panic etched across his face. "Don't make me go in there."

"It's our only option at this point."

"You don't understand," he said, voice trembling. "I *can't* go in there."

"Yes, you can. And you will," she said, her words laced with fire. "I have to take you to the cabin, and that's the only way."

Caleb sat up, dirt clinging to his back as he shot Adeline a hateful look. "I don't want to go there!"

"I don't care what you want!" she yelled. "You're going in there, even if I have to tie you to Regal."

Regal reared up and crashed his hooves into the desert floor. Dust exploded around him as he snorted hard in Caleb's face. Caleb cowered, shivering uncontrollably.

"You're getting back on Regal, and we're going in there," Adeline said, pointing to the evergreens.

Regal knelt next to Caleb, his fierce stare boring into him. Still shaking, Caleb hesitated. Then he hung his head in defeat as he remounted Regal, dragging himself into the saddle. As soon as his hands closed around the reins, Regal stood up.

Adeline huffed in frustration as she climbed back onto Angela. Rubbing the sweat from her eyes, she led the way to the evergreens. She shifted in the saddle, her muscles sore and her mind swirling. Her irritation quickly turned to unease the closer they got to the tree line.

"You have no idea the horror you're getting us into," Caleb said harshly.

Adeline ignored him, though she couldn't settle the nerves battling within her. She was heading into an unknown territory again. This time with someone she didn't trust. But she wouldn't focus on that. They were one step closer to the cabin, and that was what kept her going.

Chapter Fourteen

Prickly branches scraped against Adeline as she entered the evergreen forest. The trees stretched in every direction, all shapes and sizes blending into an ominous maze of green. It was quiet...a little too quiet.

Her mouth went dry, and her hands trembled as she searched for any signs of life.

Nothing. Not even the faintest chirp of a bird.

"We shouldn't be in here," Caleb said, barely making a sound.

Adeline scanned the woods again, battling her own fear. There were no distinct paths, just endless trees pressing in from every side. Even if there were, she wouldn't know which one to take.

"We need to head west, Angela," Adeline said to her mare. "Any idea where that is?"

Angela snorted and pressed forward through the trees with Regal following close behind. Branches smacked Adeline as they moved, every strike feeling like a warning from the forest itself. She tried to dodge them, but it was no use.

Ahead, the air seemed thicker as a pale shimmer slipped between the evergreens. The horses' steps were a little too loud for Adeline's liking, and so was Caleb's heavy breathing, as a sudden fog rolled in. It was thin at first but grew thicker with each passing second.

"Stay close," Adeline whispered.

The horses pressed on, cutting through the fog. A cool dampness filled the air, settling into her clothes and raising goosebumps along her arms. Adeline's eyes flicked left and right, searching for the boulder Henry had described. Fear prickled along her spine. She couldn't see anything; the fog had swallowed the whole forest.

"Look left."

Adeline jolted at Henry's sudden voice echoing in her head. She jerked the reins, bringing Angela to an abrupt stop. Regal nearly collided with them but stopped just in time.

Looking left, Adeline squinted at the evergreens coated in fog. The haze was too thick to make anything out. She'd have to get a closer look.

Adeline steered Angela that way, and the fog thinned just enough to reveal a cluster of spruce trees. Their dark green needles overlapped, huddled together like they were hiding something. It was too suspicious to ignore.

"Stay here." Adeline dismounted Angela.

She crept toward the trees, her heart hammering with every step. It was impossible to see past their thick, spiky limbs. She'd have to force her way through.

Sharp branches pricked her palms as she pushed them aside, stepping forward until they closed in behind her. She stumbled to a stop, nearly crashing into a boulder. Brittle vines snaked across the weathered stone, its jagged shape resembling a wolf's open mouth.

This must be it.

Adeline reached out, her shaky hand brushing the boulder's rough surface.

Assuming the secret path was behind the rock, Adeline tried to maneuver past it. But the dense pine needles refused to let her through, no matter how hard she pushed.

She knew exactly what to do.

Adeline unsheathed her dagger and began slicing the tangled branches. The scent of pine filled the air as the limbs dropped at her feet, their sound echoing unnaturally loud in the stillness of the forest.

When the last branch dropped, she paused, staring ahead. Her breath caught.

An overgrown trail stretched before her.

"I found it," she whispered.

Oak branches drooped low over the neglected trail that was overrun with weeds and briars. It was in rough shape, but the horses could handle it.

"Follow the path until you get to the fork in the road, then go right." Henry's words slipped into her mind. *"You'll be safe as long as you stay on that trail."*

"What happens if we go left?"

"You will enter the Dark Territory."

A chill swept through Adeline. *"I'll make sure we go right."*

Without wasting a second, Adeline went back the way she came, slicing through the branches that separated her from Caleb and the horses. Caleb was still quivering as she stepped out and climbed onto Angela.

"I found the path we have to take," Adeline said, navigating her mare toward the evergreens.

"Where does it go?" Caleb asked, the fear evident in his tone.

"The safe part of the forest."

"How do you know that?"

"I just do. Now let's go."

Angela moved through the roughly trimmed trees, and Regal followed. It was a tight squeeze, but they managed to push past the branches and around the boulder, entering the abandoned path.

The oak trees lining the trail were bare as though it was the dead of winter. Strands of Spanish moss dangled from their branches, slowly swaying with the unseen breeze. It was a creepy sight, especially with the fog.

"You want us to go down that?" Caleb's voice cracked.

"Yes," she said firmly. "Now be quiet."

The horses took their time trudging through the weeds and dodging the low branches. Adeline shuddered each time the overhanging moss brushed her skin. Its wispy, rough texture was aggravating but unavoidable.

Caleb ducked under a branch. "Are you sure this is the right way?"

"Yes."

Adeline had her own concerns about the rugged path. It was eerie, overgrown, and dangerously close to the Dark Territory. But she trusted Henry with her life. He would never mislead her.

"How long is this stupid path?" Caleb asked.

"I don't know." Adeline swatted away a piece of moss.

With the path being so overgrown and neglected, they were forced to move at a slower pace. Much slower than Adeline wanted. Hopefully, they'd reach the cabin before nightfall.

A gust of wind plowed into Adeline, pulling a strand of hair from her messy updo. It left as quickly as it had come.

"What was that?" Caleb asked, shuddering as he scanned the trees.

Adeline froze, unable to speak. Her eyes swept the path. Though she saw nothing through the fog, her instincts screamed that something was wrong.

"Bigsby."

The voice drifted with the wind, low and chilling.

A violent shiver shook Adeline. She knew that voice.

Ralock.

"Did you hear that?" Caleb cowered in his seat.

"Go. Now!" Adeline shouted, slamming her heels into Angela.

Angela neighed and bolted down the path, Regal charging after her. The tangled undergrowth and low-hanging tree limbs no longer mattered; their only goal was to reach the end of the path.

Adeline ducked and weaved to avoid the branches, her grip on the reins so tight her knuckles went white. Spanish moss slapped her face again and again, but she didn't care. They had to get away.

"Slow down!" Caleb screamed behind her.

Hearing nothing but the thunder of hooves beneath her, Adeline clung to the reins as the wind whipped into her. Her eyes watered, blurring her vision. She blinked hard just as the thinning fog revealed a sturdy oak branch ahead.

WHACK!

Pain exploded in Adeline's forehead. She flew off Angela and crashed onto her back. A throbbing ache pulsed through her skull as she lay stunned on the forest floor, staring up at the branches laced in fog. Caleb's panicked voice pierced the haze, but his words were a blur.

The trees spun around her as darkness closed in. She felt like she was slipping into a deep sleep as she closed her heavy eyes.

Caleb's frantic shouts faded until there was only silence.

Chapter Fifteen

Adeline's eyes fluttered open. She stared up into an umbrella of leaves, her head pounding like she'd been punched in the face. It took all her strength to rise to a sitting position. Lifting a hand to her head, she found a knot. A very big knot. Right in the middle of her forehead.

She winced as she dropped her hand and glanced around. She was no longer on the forgotten path but looked to be deep in a forest. Pine trees shot to the sky among hickory and oak trees full of vibrant green leaves.

Where am I?

Everything around her was foreign, except Angela and Regal. They were grazing on blueberries as if nothing had happened. Relief swept over her.

Then it hit her.

Where was Caleb?

She searched the wooded clearing again. No Caleb.

Great. She groaned. *He ran away.*

Adeline gritted her teeth and stood, her head pulsing as she brushed the dirt from her clothes.

I can't believe he left me. She picked a leaf from her hair. *After everything I did for him!*

A twig snapped nearby.

Adeline jumped and drew her dagger, aiming it at the dense trees. At least Caleb hadn't taken her weapon.

The footsteps grew louder, and a nearby shrub began to shake. Adeline tightened her grip. The bush parted, and out stepped a skinny boy with dreadlocks.

A moment passed before Adeline realized it was Caleb. He was wearing an entirely different outfit, like he'd just returned from a shopping trip. His dirty, ruined clothes had been replaced with a clean pair of gym shorts and a perfectly fitted T-shirt. Even his running shoes looked brand-new.

Caleb stopped when he saw Adeline, nearly dropping a handful of blackberries. "I didn't think you'd ever wake up," he said before shoving all the berries into his mouth.

Adeline lowered her weapon. "Where did you get those clothes?"

"I found them in your backpack," he said, casual as ever.

"My backpack?"

"Yeah," he said, scratching the side of his face. "I was looking for the water tin and found these clothes. I figured you wouldn't miss them."

"That doesn't make sense." Adeline sheathed her dagger. "Why would there be men's clothing in my bag?"

Caleb shrugged. "Maybe they were Jesse's."

"No offense, but Jesse's bigger than you." She eyed his bony physique. "A lot bigger."

Then it struck her. Jesse had packed her bag. He *knew* they'd run into Caleb and had packed him clothes.

Why didn't he tell me?

"Never mind about the clothes," Adeline said, surveying their surroundings. "Where are we?"

"Not sure." He gave a simple shrug. "I carried you down the path; it led us here."

Adeline arched a brow. "You carried me?"

"Yeah." His eyes dropped to his shoes. "I realized my foot was better after you fell off your horse."

Adeline's mouth hung open for a second before she closed it. That kind of kindness from Caleb was mind-boggling. "Thanks."

Caleb dipped his chin. "I owed you one for killing that snake."

Adeline had completely forgotten about the rattlesnake. Good thing she'd killed it.

"I'm a little confused." Sunlight streamed through the trees as Adeline looked around once more. "The path was supposed to take us to a fork in the road."

"It did," he said.

Adeline straightened. "Which way did you go?"

"They looked the same, so I went left."

Oh, no.

Terror plowed through her.

They were in the Dark Territory.

"We're leaving now," Adeline said, whistling for the horses.

They obeyed instantly, galloping to her side.

"Why?" Caleb cocked his head. "You said we'd be safe if we followed the trail."

"You went the wrong way!"

"I followed the path you took us down!"

"It doesn't matter." Adeline threw her hands in the air. "We're in a *very* dangerous place and have to go!"

A dark presence rolled in like a storm, suffocating the air around them. Adeline knew it was Ralock before he even stepped into the clearing, dressed in a tailored black suit. Thin streaks of gold swayed along the fabric as he puffed out his chest.

"Well, look who it is," Ralock said, a wicked smirk curling on his lips.

Adeline staggered back, her breath stolen by sheer horror.

Ralock looked exactly as she remembered. Tall, dark, and handsome, except for the scar running down the left side of his face. It started beneath his eye and went all the way to his jaw. It was discolored and noticeable against his tan complexion, but it only added to his charming looks.

"My, how you have grown, Bigsby."

Hearing her last name roll off his tongue made Adeline cringe. She grabbed her bow from Angela's saddle, reached over her head for an arrow, and nocked it in one swift motion. Drawing the bowstring tight, she aimed the arrow tip at his chest. "Get back!"

Dark laughter rumbled from Ralock. "Is that supposed to scare me?"

He stood about thirty yards away. An easy target.

Adeline held her breath, fear prickling her skin as she let the arrow fly.

It sliced through the air, zeroing in on his heart.

But just before impact, Ralock reached out and caught it. He looked unimpressed as he slammed it against his thigh, snapping it in half. He tossed the pieces into the woods.

"Now, that's no way to greet an old friend," he said, crossing his arms as a breeze stirred his short black hair.

Blood rushed from Adeline's face as she slowly lowered her bow. He'd caught her arrow in midair like a slow pitch.

Her heart hammered. She needed an escape plan...fast.

Although tempted to mount Angela and flee, Adeline couldn't abandon Caleb. She'd made a promise to Jesse and would keep it no matter what.

"Caleb," Adeline whispered urgently, "get on Regal."

Caleb stood transfixed, shivering as he stared at Ralock.

"Caleb." She reached out, gently touching his arm.

He flinched, his lips quivering. "He found me."

"What?"

"I hate to intrude on your little party, but I'm here to claim what's mine," Ralock said, his voice smooth and mocking as he focused on Caleb. "Come here, Caleb."

Adeline couldn't breathe as the horrifying truth sank in. Caleb's cruel master was Ralock. No wonder he was so mean.

"If I go with you," Caleb said, his shoulders stiffening, "will you leave Adeline alone?"

An evil smirk tugged at Ralock's thin lips. "You strike a hard bargain, boy."

"Do we have a deal?" Caleb asked, trembling all over.

Ralock placed a hand over his heart. "I promise I will not lay a hand on her."

Caleb took a step forward.

"Don't." Adeline grabbed his arm. "He will kill you."

"I'm already a dead man," he said. "Save yourself."

"I'm not leaving you."

"Get out of here." Caleb ripped free from her grip.

Adeline's hand fell to her side; she could only watch as Caleb shuffled toward Ralock, his head hung low. Once he was by his side, Ralock flung an arm around Caleb's scrawny shoulders like they were old pals. They were nearly the same height, but Caleb looked like a kid next to Ralock's fit physique.

"Kill her," Ralock said, his words cracking like a whip.

Two military men stepped from the trees behind Ralock. They'd been there the whole time. Their camouflaged faces and dark green armor had hidden them well.

A long shiver rippled down Adeline's back as she met their sinister yellow eyes. The longer she looked, the more certain she was that they were not human. They were identical in every way, as if they'd been cloned. From their bald heads to their tall stature, everything was the same. Even the way they stood, watching her.

Escaping came to mind again. She could easily leave. But what about Caleb? He would die if she left him.

"You said you would leave her alone." Caleb slammed into Ralock, trying to break free.

"I said *I* wouldn't touch her," Ralock said. He laughed wickedly as he dug his claw-like nails into Caleb's shoulders. "I never said anything about my hunters."

An agonizing scream tore from Caleb as he tried to escape. He thrashed and twisted his thin frame, but it was no use. Ralock was too strong.

"Run, Adeline!" he cried.

"Aw, isn't that adorable?" Ralock's nails dug deeper into Caleb's flesh. "Who knew you could care about anyone but yourself?"

A steady stream of blood trickled down Caleb's arm as he whimpered in defeat and stopped struggling.

Adeline pinched her lips shut, rage coiling in her core. She dropped her bow and drew her dagger, the glass blade shimmering against the sunlight. Although she disliked Caleb, she wouldn't let Ralock kill him.

She pointed the blade straight at Ralock. "Let him go."

Ralock threw his head back in laughter, and the soldiers joined in. "You're way out of your element here, Bigsby. This is *my* land; I control everything and everyone in it."

Adeline stood between Regal and Angela, her stomach churning. Despite her terror, she maintained a brave face.

The two hunters unsheathed their jagged swords. Adeline paled. She'd seen those solid black blades before. Memories of the Loydaya tunnel flashed before her. Ralock had wielded a sword just like that...and so had Caleb when they'd first met.

Adeline silently kicked herself for not putting the pieces together, but now was not the time to think about it.

"Let's make this a little more interesting," Ralock said with a slick smile. He raised his free hand and twisted it in the air until black dust swirled around his fingers. The dust widened and shifted before him like a cloud until a pack of wolverines materialized. There were twelve of them, hissing and gnashing their teeth as they awaited their master's instructions.

"Kill her and bring me that dagger."

Terror seized Adeline, freezing her to the spot. How was she supposed to fight them all? There were too many.

"Tell the horses to kill the wolverines." Jesse's calm voice drifted through her thoughts. *"You focus on the hunters."*

"There are two of them!"

"You're ready for this," he said. *"Stand your ground."*

Adeline watched the approaching threat, her fear intensifying. The hunters crouched as they snuck behind the wolverines with weapons in hand. They walked silently, their yellow eyes fixed on her.

She buried the rising panic.

"Kill the wolverines," she whispered to Regal and Angela. "I'll handle the men."

Neighing, Regal reared up on his hind legs before charging at the wolverines. Angela followed his lead, slamming her hooves into the earth. The wolverines met them in the middle, and the two sides collided.

Chaos erupted. The horses held their ground, kicking and stomping the vicious animals that tore into their flesh. Blood spewed through the air, but the horses didn't back down.

Adeline's gut twisted. She desperately wanted to help them, but she had to focus on the hunters heading her way. They crept in unison, their alligator eyes locked on Adeline as they looked her up and down. Goosebumps crawled from her neck to her toes. She'd never faced anything like them. Their painted faces and reptilian eyes were intimidating, but they were no bigger than Jesse. She'd had plenty of practice with him. Plus, her dagger could easily pierce their light armor.

I can do this.

"She's nothing but a child," one of them said in a low, haunting voice.

"An easy kill," the other hissed with a vicious grin. "Let me handle her."

Another round of chills shot through Adeline as the cocky hunter strutted forward while the other stayed back to watch.

He wasted no time and swung at her chest. She jumped out of the way, bark scraping her arm as she skimmed past a tree. He bared his teeth and came back with another hard swing. She leaped back, the blade hissing past her ribs.

"Kill the girl," the watching hunter snarled.

"I'm trying."

A horrific roar ripped from the hunter as he launched another attack, only to be blocked by Adeline's dagger.

Clang!

Sparks burst as their blades clashed.

Confusion crossed the hunter's face. He shoved forward, knocking Adeline off balance as the weapons separated.

She had barely recovered before the next strike.

Adeline ducked, the blade swishing over her head.

Gritting her teeth, Adeline rose and drove the tip of her blade into the hunter's chest. A vicious scream tore from his throat as she twisted the blade. He went limp, dead before he hit the ground.

Adeline tugged her weapon free from his leather armor. Before she had a chance to recover, a hand fisted her hair and yanked her backward. She thrashed and screamed as the second hunter dragged her across the forest floor, away from the one she'd killed.

He cursed and dropped her hard, slamming his boot into her side.

Pain seared in her ribs as she curled forward. He kicked her again and again, his thick boot pounding into her back like a battering ram. She gasped for air, helpless to stop him.

"Help me, Jesse!" she screamed.

The hunter paused and laughed alongside Ralock, who was enjoying the show.

"Yell louder," Ralock said, still clutching Caleb by his side. "I'm sure he'll hear you."

As their taunts echoed around her, Jesse's voice cut through the noise in her mind. *"Sit up and stab your dagger into the ground in front of you."*

"That's a terrible idea!"

"Trust me."

Adeline winced as she dragged herself into a sitting position. The hunter loomed above her with soulless eyes. He raised his sword above her head, ready to pierce her skull.

"Now!" Jesse instructed.

Adeline plunged the dagger into the dirt right as the hunter's blade came down. A blue force field burst to life, wrapping around her like a protective bubble. The sword struck it—

BOOM!

A shockwave blasted from the shield, hurling the hunter as if he'd stepped on a landmine. He slammed into a tree, where a splintered branch pierced his chest. He hung there motionless, suspended above the ground.

The shield vanished, and Adeline pushed herself to her feet, her back thumping with pain.

Whoa.

She did a slow circle, her dagger sweeping the area. It looked like a war zone. Several trees had been knocked over, while some had been thrown across the forest. Even a handful of shrubs had been ripped from the ground.

Angela and Regal stood among the disorder, licking their wounds. They were covered in blood, but at least they were alive. The wolverines weren't so lucky. Blood pooled beneath their mangled bodies before they slowly disappeared.

Did that blast kill them too?

Adeline shook the thought away. She had to focus. Caleb needed her.

She searched the destruction, her pulse hammering as her eyes swept over tangled trees. A flicker of movement in the distance made her look twice. Someone was struggling beneath a fallen tree limb.

Caleb.

She hobbled toward him but skidded to a stop when she saw black hair. Ralock shoved the limb off his chest and struggled to rise. Clutching his side, he limped into the forest, disappearing into the trees. He'd be back soon...with reinforcements.

Adeline had to find Caleb. Fast.

"Caleb!" Adeline rushed to the spot where Ralock had been. "Where are you?"

No response.

Panic set in as Adeline tore through the debris, slicing and tossing limbs aside. She yanked a shrub from her path. And there he was, lying beneath it.

He was motionless, his eyes closed.

He's dead.

Stashing her dagger, Adeline dropped to her knees and grabbed his shirt. "Wake up!"

He remained still.

"Don't you dare die on me!" She shook him.

A low moan escaped Caleb's lips as his eyes fluttered open. Fright and confusion swirled in his golden-green irises. "How did you do that?" he asked, his voice cracking.

"No clue." Adeline sank back into the dirt. "I just did what Jesse told me to do."

"Jesse?" Caleb sat up. "Where is he?"

"He's not here."

"Then how did you talk to him?"

"I can communicate with him through my thoughts," Adeline said, gently rubbing the knot on her forehead.

Caleb stared at her blankly; he clearly didn't believe her.

"I'm serious," she said.

"You're saying you can telepathically talk to Jesse?"

"Yes. Anytime, anywhere."

"Sure you can," he muttered.

Although the urge to retaliate was strong, Adeline held her tongue as Caleb slowly rolled up his blood-soaked sleeve. Deep puncture wounds and a faded scar marred his thin shoulder. Her heart sank. She could only imagine the abuse he'd endured living in that dreadful place.

"Do you have any more bandages?" Caleb asked, wincing as he pulled his sleeve higher.

Adeline leaned in for a better look and cringed. It looked like a bear had gripped him. She hadn't realized just how lethal Ralock's nails were.

Her hand instinctively went to her dagger, then stopped. Jesse had told her not to use it on Caleb.

"Seal them up." Jesse entered her thoughts.

"I thought you didn't want me to use my dagger on him."

"He would've run if we'd healed his ankle with it. He's ready now."

Things started to click for Adeline. Of course Caleb would've bolted if her dagger had healed his foot. Jesse had known that and deliberately slowed the healing to ensure Caleb would go with her to the cabin.

"This is going to sound crazy." Adeline grabbed her dagger, sparkles shimmering within the glass blade. "But I'm going to seal your wounds with this."

Caleb cocked a brow. "Excuse me?"

"You heard me."

He scurried to his feet. "No way am I letting you get near me with that thing."

"It'll only take a second."

"Leave me alone." Caleb backed away. "I'm fine."

"You are *not* fine." Adeline went after him.

"Back off!"

Adeline rubbed her temple. "You're the most difficult person I've ever met."

"Right back at you!"

"You're making this harder than it needs to be," Adeline said through gritted teeth. "If you'd just stand still, I can heal your shoulder and we can leave."

Caleb crossed his arms. "I don't believe you."

"I'm telling the truth."

"Prove it."

Adeline's nostrils flared. "Fine."

Extending her arm, Adeline pressed the dagger against her forearm. The sting made her flinch, but she didn't stop until she drew blood. Then she flipped the blade and pressed the flat side to the cut.

A quick surge of heat pulsed into her skin. It was uncomfortable at first, but the pain faded, replaced by a soothing warmth.

Adeline lifted her weapon and held out her arm to Caleb. "See? I told you."

"What the..." Caleb's eyes widened as he leaned in, searching for the cut that was no longer there. "How does it do that?"

"Not sure how, but it can." Adeline grabbed his elbow. "Now hold still."

Caleb trembled but stayed put as Adeline held the glass blade above his injured shoulder.

"This is going to burn a little," she said, tightening her grip on his arm, "so brace yourself."

Caleb recoiled when the blade touched his wounds. Groaning, he tried to pull away, but she held him steady until he relaxed.

"Done." Adeline lifted the weapon.

Caleb stepped back and touched his shoulder. His mouth opened in shock as he smeared away the blood. The wounds were completely gone, leaving no trace that he'd ever been touched. "I need to get one of those," he said, rolling down his soiled sleeve.

"Good luck with that." Adeline sheathed her weapon. "We need to get moving before Ralock comes back."

"I agree." Caleb scanned the wreckage. "I don't recognize this area, but I bet we're in the red zone."

"Red zone?" Adeline asked. "What does that mean?"

"It means we're in danger." Caleb headed toward the horses. "The hunters patrol the red zone."

"I don't even know what that is." Adeline trailed behind him, pain firing up her back.

"I don't have time to explain it to you," Caleb said as he stepped over a fallen tree. "We have to leave now."

Adeline wanted to know more, but Caleb was right. They needed to leave before more trouble showed up.

My bow!

She stopped short, scanning the disorderly ground. It could be anywhere.

"I need to find my bow first," she said, picking up a leafy limb.

Caleb turned around. "I'll help."

Together, they rummaged through piles of leaves and broken branches. Adeline fought the urge to groan as she bent to move a shrub. The pain in her back was excruciating now that the adrenaline had passed.

"Why don't you heal yourself with that dagger?" Caleb asked, heaving a large branch aside.

"It doesn't work on bruises," Adeline said, tossing another limb. "Only cuts."

"Why?"

"Beats me." Adeline tugged the brush up and gasped. Her bow was staring up at her, perfectly intact. She plunged her hand into the tangled mess, the limbs scratching at her skin as she pulled up her bow. She held it up. "Got it!"

"Good. Let's go." Caleb led the way to the horses, who were still nursing their wounds.

Adeline lagged behind, her body throbbing with each step, but she didn't voice any complaints as she reached Angela.

"You okay, pretty girl?" she asked.

Angela dipped her head gently, but the gash on her leg said otherwise. Blood poured from the cut, staining her white coat.

Adeline quickly hooked her bow to the saddle before using her dagger to heal Angela's wound. The gash sealed, then disappeared. There were a few other scratches, but nothing detrimental. She would worry about those later. She went to Regal and did the same thing.

When both horses were as good as new, she mounted Angela and turned to Caleb, who was already on Regal. "Do you remember how to get back to that path we were on?"

"Yeah," Caleb said, flicking the reins. "Follow me."

He led the way through the uprooted trees and bushes that polluted the area while Adeline bit back a moan. Her bruised, battered body cried out in protest as she rocked atop the saddle. She hoped the cabin was close.

"Do not go that way." Henry's gentle accent drifted into her thoughts.

"Why?" Adeline asked, her discomfort increasing with each shift in the saddle.

"Ralock is setting up an ambush."

Her stomach churned. *"Where do we go?"*

"You'll have to navigate through the Dark Territory."

The air escaped her chest. *"I know nothing about this place."*

"Caleb does."

"He said he doesn't recognize this area."

"Follow the dove," Henry said. *"It will take you in the right direction."*

A sudden flash of white darted past Adeline. She jumped, her heart pattering as she searched the trees.

A beautiful dove bounced on a nearby branch, watching her. Now that it had Adeline's attention, it shot from the tree, heading in the opposite direction. Glancing back, Adeline found the dove hovering over a different footpath.

"Stop!" Adeline pulled on the reins.

The horses halted, and Caleb jolted forward. He managed to stay in the saddle, his eyes wide with alarm as he twisted to face her. "What's wrong?"

"We can't go that way."

"Why not?"

"Ralock's setting up an ambush on that path."

Caleb spun Regal around. "How could you possibly know that?"

"Because my friend Henry just told me," Adeline said, no longer caring whether he believed her or not.

A look of confusion crossed his face. "Henry Snow?"

Adeline blinked, startled. She hadn't considered that Caleb might know Henry too. A dozen questions sparked in her mind, but they'd have to wait. There were more pressing matters at hand.

"Yes," she said, pointing behind her. "And he told me to follow that dove."

Caleb followed her finger to the bird circling above a narrow footpath, its white wings bright against the trees. "You want us to follow a bird? You're insane."

"No, I'm not. If we want to survive, we have to go that way."

"That'll take us deeper into the territory!"

"I know it sounds crazy," she said, keeping her voice even, "but it's our only chance."

"Nope." He shook his head. "I'm going the way we came."

"Fine." She threw up a hand. "If you want to walk into Ralock's trap, be my guest. But I'm going down that path, and Regal's coming with me."

Caleb's face reddened, his lips pressing into a hard line as Adeline turned Angela around. His glare burned into her back as she guided her mare toward the waiting dove.

The bird hovered above the trail, its wings slow and steady, like it had all the time in the world.

Angela stopped at the mouth of the narrow path. It was heavily guarded by hickory trees, untouched by the blast. Their thick, leafy branches hid the path's length.

A moment later, Regal trotted up beside her.

Adeline shifted in the saddle and glanced at Caleb. He refused to look at her, his arms locked tightly over his chest.

"You're going to get us killed," he said coldly.

Adeline rolled her eyes and pressed her heels into Angela's sides. Pain knifed through her bruised body, but she clenched her jaw and stayed upright. She kept her gaze ahead, refusing to let Caleb or the pain slow her down.

Here we go.

Chapter Sixteen

The dove flew ahead, gliding through the air like it was pleased to be their guide. It moved at a steady pace, weaving between branches with effortless grace. The horses easily followed it, their hooves crunching along the dry earth.

Adeline rocked in the saddle, pushing past the ache in her ribs as she scanned the woods around her.

Sunlight dappled through the vibrant leaves, casting golden patches across the trail. It looked peaceful, but peace was the last thing Adeline felt.

Now that she knew they were inside Ralock's territory, a chill of fear crept up her spine and refused to leave. Where were they headed? Would Ralock find them again? And if he did...what then?

"Why didn't you run when you had the chance?" Caleb asked, looking ahead as he rode by her side.

"Because I promised Jesse I'd take you to his cabin. So that's what I'm going to do."

He was quiet for a moment. "Why does he want me to go there?"

"I don't know."

The dove drifted farther down the trail, vanishing around a curve. Adeline tensed as they followed. When they rounded the bend, the path stretched ahead again, curving toward yet another corner. There was no end in sight.

Adeline searched the forest for signs of danger, but her thoughts kept returning to Caleb. Question after question swirled around her mind. How did he know Ralock? Had he been captured?

Seeing him with Ralock did something to her. She wasn't sure if it was compassion or righteous anger. Maybe both.

She still didn't like Caleb, but she had a better understanding of why he acted the way he did. His harsh and angry demeanor was probably his way of protecting himself.

No wonder he'd tried to kill her a couple of days ago; he hadn't known any better.

"Who were those creepy guys with Ralock?" Adeline asked as the horses went around the bend. "I've never seen anything like them."

"They're called hunters. They're part of Ralock's military."

"Why are they called that?"

"Because they hunt people down," he said, casting her a quick look.

Adeline swallowed hard. She hoped she never saw one of them again.

"Earlier you mentioned a red zone," she said. "What does that mean?"

"Here's a quick lesson for you," Caleb said, his eyes darting from tree to tree. "There are two zones in the Dark Territory: red and white. The red zone runs along the border. Only Ralock's military is allowed there. If you get caught there, you'll be punished."

"And the white zone?" she asked.

"That's the center of the land," he said. "Ralock's followers are free to roam there. It's supposed to be neutral, but it's still dangerous."

Adeline frowned. She'd never heard of such a thing. "Who are Ralock's followers?"

Caleb gave her a pointed look. "Are you really that clueless?"

"I've never been here before," she said firmly. "All I know is that this place belongs to Ralock, and it's dangerous."

Caleb gave a faint scoff. "No wonder you're so naive about traveling through it."

"I'm just doing what I'm told," Adeline said with a touch of sass in her tone. "It would be helpful if you'd tell me about this place. The more I know, the better chance we have of escaping."

Caleb studied her for a long moment. "Anyone with this tattoo is one of Ralock's followers." He extended his arm, showing her the black cobra inked into his skin. "Once you have this mark, you can't leave. If you try, Ralock's hunters will hunt you down, beat you, and drag you back."

Adeline's skin prickled. Her gaze locked onto the twisting snake. It was no surprise that it had creeped her out the first time she saw it. "So...anyone with that tattoo is basically Ralock's slave?"

"Yeah," Caleb said. "Not exactly sure how it works, but the more people who have it, the stronger he gets."

"Why would you ever want to be one of his followers?" she asked. "He's a monster."

"He tricked me," Caleb mumbled, barely audible.

Adeline waited for an explanation; she didn't get one.

What was his life like here?

One look at him showed that it must've been horrific. The poor hygiene, the sickly frame, the scars. It was clear he'd been through something terrible. She didn't need the details to know he'd been abused.

Adeline tried to imagine what he was like before Ralock.

Was he nice? Funny? she thought. *Or was he always a jerk with a bad temper?*

Shaking him from her mind, she scolded herself. She had to stop thinking about him and focus.

A warm breeze caressed her face as the dove glided down the path, weaving through the thick forest. The trail curved, and something strange caught her eye.

Sand.

She rubbed her eyes, but the sand was still there. It blanketed the forest floor, stretching into the trees.

Why would there be sand in a forest?

The horses slowed their pace as they navigated through the thick sand that took over the woods. It wasn't long before the trail disappeared altogether.

Adeline broke through the tree line, and a light hit her like a wave. She lifted a hand, blinking against the brightness. When her eyes adjusted, she drew in a breath.

A crystal lake dominated the view, surrounded by pine trees that spread into the forest. Sunlight sparkled against the water as gentle waves lapped onto the shore.

"Wow." Adeline pulled the reins, stopping Angela. "I didn't expect to see this."

Regal stepped up beside Angela while Caleb anxiously looked every which way. "Something isn't right about this place."

Ignoring his remark, Adeline slid off Angela. An ache flared across her body as she straightened, a quiet reminder of the beating she'd endured earlier. She dug through her backpack and pulled out an empty water tin.

"I'm going to fill up on water." Adeline walked toward the shoreline. "I don't want us to run out."

Caleb stayed on Regal, fidgeting with the reins. "I've got a bad feeling about this place."

"This'll just take a second," she said without turning.

"I'm serious. We should go."

Adeline rolled her eyes and kept moving. She didn't have time for his paranoia. It was just water. And they needed it.

"Don't touch the water!" Caleb yelled.

Adeline ignored him yet again and kept walking.

Out of nowhere, something crashed into her back. She hit the ground hard, face-first in the sand. The water tin flew from her grip as Caleb landed on top of her with a grunt.

Pain seared up her back as she spat out a mouthful of sand. "Get off me!"

Caleb rolled off, gasping for air as he scrambled to his feet.

"What's your problem?" Adeline pushed herself up and got in his face, her fists clenched. She was ready to deck him.

Caleb bent over, hands on his knees, wheezing. "The water...the water is..."

"The water is what, Caleb?"

He looked up, pale-faced. "Poisonous."

Adeline let out a disbelieving laugh and flung a hand toward the water. "You think that pretty lake is poisonous?"

Caleb shook his head, still breathing heavily. "The whole thing...It's acid."

Her stomach dropped. "How do you know that?"

"You probably wouldn't believe it," he said, brushing the sand off his gym shorts.

"Try me." She planted her hands on her hips.

Caleb glanced away, awkwardly tapping his fingers against his thigh. "Sometimes I get visions of the past. Or the future."

"Visions?" she asked with a raised brow.

"Yeah. They started when I first came to this world." He stared down at his sand-covered shoes. "They come out of nowhere; it's like I see flashes of pictures in my mind that I can't control."

"That's weird."

"I knew you wouldn't believe me."

"I didn't say I didn't believe you. I just said it was weird." She'd never had a vision, but anything was possible in that realm. "What did you see?"

"I saw Ralock throwing people into that lake," he said, casting a haunted look toward the water. "As soon as their bodies touched it, their skin melted like wax. They were screaming as they tried to swim to shore, but they didn't make it."

Adeline's eyes went wide. "You saw all that in your head?"

"Yeah."

"That's crazy." She started toward the water. "Let's see if it's true."

Caleb snatched her wrist, tugging her to a stop. "Are you insane?"

"I'm not going to touch it, dummy." Adeline shook him off. "I'm tossing in a stick."

Caleb stayed rigid, his breathing shallow, as Adeline plucked a stick from the sand and hurled it into the shimmering lake.

The moment it hit the surface, it hissed. Smoke curled from it like it had been dipped in fire. It disintegrated in seconds.

A cold chill slid down Adeline's neck.

That could have been me.

She turned to Caleb. "You were right. It's poisonous."

Caleb didn't answer, his focus solely on the lake. There was sorrow in his eyes, as if he could feel the pain of what he'd seen.

Another ounce of sympathy grew in Adeline. He didn't have to stop her from touching the water...but he did. Maybe he wasn't so bad after all.

"Thanks," she said softly, brushing past him to retrieve the water tin.

Caleb didn't respond. He just followed her back to the horses, his steps quiet behind hers.

The dove sat perched on Angela's saddle, blinking at Adeline once before lifting into the air. It glided across the sand to another section of the woods.

Adeline tucked the water tin away, eager to get moving.

"You need to move on without the horses." Henry's voice filled her thoughts.

Her heart stopped. *"Tell me you're joking."*

"I'm not," Henry said calmly. *"You'll be spotted if you take them with you."*

"What if Ralock finds us again?" Adeline started to sweat. *"We need their protection."*

"I need you to trust me," he said. *"Send the horses away and follow the dove."*

Fear tangled her thoughts as she rubbed her temples. Leaving the horses was the last thing she wanted to do, but she trusted Henry.

She exhaled slowly, bracing herself. Caleb wasn't going to be happy. She glanced over at him. "We aren't taking the horses with us."

Caleb's hands froze on the saddle as he tried to climb up. "What did you say?"

"We can't take them any farther."

"Are you delusional? We need them if we want to escape this territory!"

"Henry just told me we'll be spotted if we bring them."

Caleb threw up his hands. "There you go again with the whole Henry thing."

"You have no room to talk, *Mister I-Have-Visions.*"

"We need them!" he barked, spit flinging from his mouth. "You have *no* idea how hard it is to get out of here."

"I don't want to go on without them either," she said, raising her voice, "but I trust Henry. He told me to move on without the horses, and that's exactly what we're going to do."

Caleb balled his fists like he was about to hit her. Instead, he stormed off, cursing under his breath. He didn't go far before dropping to the sand.

Closing her eyes, Adeline gently kneaded her achy forehead. Just when she thought Caleb wasn't so bad...

A gentle nudge startled her. Angela was there, her bright blue eyes searching Adeline's. She must've heard them.

Adeline leaned forward and pressed her forehead to the mare's. "You and Regal have to go back to the garden without us."

Angela snorted and jerked back her head, shaking it fiercely. Even Regal stomped in protest.

"Stop," Adeline said sternly. "I'll be fine, but you two need to go now."

The horses glanced at one another, debating what to do.

Whish!

The wind of an arrow zoomed past Adeline's head and slammed into the sand beside her.

Time stood still as she snatched her bow from Angela's saddle and spun around. Panic burst inside her.

A band of hunters emerged from the woods near the lake. It was hard to see how many there were—their green armor and camouflaged faces blended in with the trees, but she counted at least four of them.

Another arrow flew straight toward her.

Before Adeline could react, Angela lunged in front of her.

The arrow struck the horse, and Adeline screamed. Her hand flew to her mouth. It was lodged deep in her mare's side, and blood immediately soaked her white coat.

With a grunt, Angela bit down on the arrow and snapped it in half before shooting Adeline an intense look. She neighed loudly in her face as if telling her to run.

"I can't leave you," Adeline cried, her vision clouding with tears.

"You must leave." Henry's voice thundered in her mind. *"They'll be fine."*

The ground rumbled as Regal charged toward the hunters. He rammed into one who'd just stepped out of the trees, sending him sprawling. Before the man could recover, Regal trampled him to death. Without hesitation, the stallion turned his fury on the next hunter.

Angela gave Adeline one last look before storming toward the fight. She galloped through the sand like she hadn't been wounded, her purple-streaked mane whipping in the wind.

"Get Caleb and follow the dove!" Henry's voice snapped Adeline back to reality.

Adeline spun around and spotted Caleb running in the opposite direction. Sand flung behind him as he raced toward the trees where the dove was waiting. Bow in hand, she ran after him. Every muscle ached as she pushed forward.

She couldn't lose him. Not now.

She pumped her arms and forced herself to go faster, her body screaming in agony as Caleb disappeared into the forest.

As she neared the narrow path, the dove launched into flight, swooping past Caleb as he ran.

Branches slapped against Adeline's arms and shoulders as she gained on him. She could hear his ragged exhales even before she caught up with him.

Slowing to a jog, Adeline stayed a few steps ahead of Caleb, her eyes trained on the dove. Now and then, it glanced back as if it was checking on them before darting deeper down the narrow path.

They ran until the only thing that could be heard was their heavy breathing.

"I think we're safe for now," Adeline said, slowing to a walk.

Caleb matched her strides, his hands braced on his hips as he struggled to breathe. He moved like his feet were made of lead, and Adeline worried he might collapse.

Now that the adrenaline had faded, she realized how bad their situation was.

No supplies. No water. No horses.

She shoved her hand into her pockets, searching for anything useful. All she felt was the old pocket watch from the desert.

She sighed. They were in trouble. At least she still had her weapons.

"Let's take a break," Adeline said, running a hand across her forehead.

Caleb sank down without saying a word. Sweat dripped from his dirty face, and his cheeks flushed red as his chest heaved with every shallow inhale.

The dove stopped as well, settling on a nearby limb.

Adeline moved a short distance away before sitting down. Pain racked her body as she leaned back against a tree, trying to ignore the dryness in her throat. She longed to rest, but that wasn't an option. They couldn't stay there long.

"Are you okay?" she asked as sweat trickled down her face.

Caleb answered with a shrug.

"Hopefully we'll make it to the cabin before nightfall," she said, glancing at the dove to make sure it was still there.

"Don't get your hopes up."

Adeline pinched her dry lips together and shook her head. "Do you always have to be so negative?"

"I'm realistic," he said, his breathing starting to slow. "I've been here long enough to know that it's impossible to escape Ralock. He always finds you."

"That might be your experience with Ralock," she said, "but it's not mine."

"Why aren't you afraid of him?"

"I am afraid of him," she said, tucking a stray piece of hair behind her ear.

"You don't act like it."

"Well, I am. He almost killed me last year, but I got away."

"How?"

"I hit him in the face with my dagger."

Caleb studied her for a moment. "Are you the one who gave him that scar?"

Adeline shrugged. "I guess."

"I remember the day he got it," he said, looking off to the side. "He was livid. His healers tried to stitch him up; they didn't do a great job."

"He wasn't the only one left with a scar." She brushed a finger over the mark on her thigh. "I'm just glad mine isn't on my face."

Caleb glanced at the two-inch scar above her knee. "What happened?"

"Ralock threw a knife at me."

Caleb's face folded into a frown as he grabbed a handful of dead pine needles and began to pull them apart. He avoided her gaze, tossing each piece aside. "I know all about those knives."

Sadness bloomed in Adeline as she watched him. From where she sat, she could make out a few of his scars, but she was sure there were more hidden beneath his shirt. She wanted to know how he got them but didn't want to intrude. Maybe one day he'd tell her.

"We'd better go," she said, placing a hand on her lower back as she stood.

Pain fired up her frame as she did a quick stretch. She desperately needed a longer break. So did Caleb. She wasn't sure how much more his feeble body could take, but they had to keep moving.

The dove shot from the tree, the limb bouncing from its departure. It twirled along the path, happily showing them the way. Sighing, Adeline dragged her weary legs after it.

Chapter Seventeen

THE SMELL OF PINE hung in the air as Adeline and Caleb followed the dove down the winding path. It weaved and curved through the woods, with no visible end. The pleasant scent lingered even after the pine trees gave way to a forest of oak and hickory trees. Their long, protective limbs shadowed the trail, shielding them from the sun.

Adeline swiped the sweat from her face. She was already drenched. So was Caleb. His clothes clung to him as if he'd been tossed in a lake.

They needed shelter. And water. Soon.

"Where did you stay when you lived here?" she asked, walking beside him. "Did you sleep outside?"

"No. There's a big city in the middle of the territory," he said, pushing a limb out of the way. "Most of Ralock's followers live there."

"There's a city here? What's it like?"

"It's like the cities back home," he said, "but more dangerous. More corrupt. Everyone either wants to kill you or steal from you."

Adeline shook her head. "I had no idea."

"Nothing here is safe," he said, not sparing her a glance. "That's why most followers try to leave."

"But they can't?"

"The hunters patrol the border. They're trackers—good ones. Escaping is almost impossible."

"Then how did you get out?"

"I got lucky. Or so I thought," he said, his tone as hard as his expression. "It doesn't matter now. I'm right back where I started."

"I'm sorry, Caleb," she said quietly. "I can't imagine how hard this is for you."

"I don't want your sympathy." He threw her a cold look. "I want to get out of this hellhole and never come back."

"I'm going to get us out of here."

"That's what they all say," he said with an eye roll.

A distant sound drifted with the wind. Adeline froze. It sounded like muffled voices mixed with machinery.

Caleb heard it too. He stood like a statue next to her, his muscles taut. "What was that?"

"I'm not sure," she said as the dove fluttered down onto a branch above them.

There was a small clearing ahead, and Adeline knew what she had to do. "Stay here."

She snuck toward the clearing. The noise grew louder the closer she got to the steep ledge. When she caught sight of the view below, her heart started pounding in her chest.

It was a large city tucked against the base of a mountain. Brick homes, winding roads, and buildings went as far as she could see. People and animals drifted through the streets like ants in a distant maze.

"What do you see?" Caleb asked, his voice hushed.

"It's a city." Adeline glanced back at him.

Caleb rushed to her side, his face draining of color as he stared down at the city. His hands trembled at his sides. "Why are we here?" he demanded, whipping his head toward her. "This is the worst place we could be."

"I don't know yet," she said, keeping her tone even, "but getting upset with me won't help."

Caleb paced the clearing, jamming his fingers into his tangled dreadlocks. "I knew I shouldn't have followed you."

"Then why did you?" she asked with a murderous look. "Your foot's better now."

"I don't have a choice." He stepped in close, his breath hot with anger. "The only way out of here is with a weapon, and *you* broke mine."

"Well, maybe if you hadn't tried to kill me, you'd still have your stupid sword."

Caw! Caw!

A massive black crow soared above the trees, circling the area.

Caleb shoved Adeline back. She slammed into an oak tree, his hand clamping over her mouth as he pinned her in place.

Adeline screamed into his palm, bucking against him in a wild panic.

"Shut up," he hissed, pressing closer. "It'll hear you."

Adeline stopped struggling as the crow shrieked overhead. Luckily, the thick branches concealed them. Her lungs burned as she held her breath, fighting the urge to gag. Caleb smelled disgusting. No wonder he was friends with wolves; he smelled just like them.

Seconds dragged by like minutes. Adeline wasn't sure she could stay put much longer. Finally, the crow moved on, its cries more distant than before.

"The crows patrol the territory." Caleb removed his hand and stepped back. "I'm positive that one was looking for you."

Adeline shivered at the thought as she adjusted her tank top. Brushing past him, she poked her head out and glanced around. No sign of the crow.

She turned back to Caleb with a fierce look. "Do you want to leave this territory with me or not?"

Caleb met her stare, the muscles in his neck pulsing.

"Answer me."

"Yes," he said through gritted teeth.

"Then keep your mouth shut. No more rude comments. No more arguing. Can you handle that?"

Caleb pressed his lips together and gave a quick nod.

"Good," she said. "Let's keep going."

Adeline stepped back onto the path, searching all around for the dove. It wasn't there. Maybe it fled when the crow appeared.

Adeline exhaled, rubbing her achy head. They didn't have time to wait for it to come back; they had to act now.

"Henry, what do we do?" she asked through her thoughts.

"Caleb knows the way," Henry said plainly.

"That doesn't answer my question."

Silence. Absolute silence.

Groaning in frustration, Adeline rubbed a hand down her sweaty face. She hated when her friends did that. She looked at Caleb. Like it or not, she needed his help. "How well do you know this area?"

"I'd say pretty well, considering I used to live in that city," he said, focusing on the activity below.

She stiffened and stared at him. "You lived there?"

"Yep."

"Do you know where the cabin is from here?"

"It's on the other side of that mountain," he said, pointing to the towering range that scraped the sky. "The only way there is through the tunnel in the city."

Adeline quickly found the tunnel and felt sick. Soldiers in black tactical gear guarded the entrance. She knew exactly who they were...warriors. The last time she'd faced one had been a disaster. There was no way she could take on an entire group of them now. "There has to be another way."

"Trust me, there isn't."

Adeline ignored him and tapped her chin. She studied the city, then shifted her eyes to the wooded mountain. As she scanned the trees, something shiny caught the sunlight. It was high in elevation and appeared to be some kind of structure, partially hidden by the thick forest canopy.

"What's that?" she asked, pointing.

Caleb shaded his eyes. "That's the abandoned mine. It caved in years ago."

An ember of hope sparked in her. "Did the tunnels lead to the other side of the mountain?"

"I think so."

"Do you think we could get there without being noticed?"

"Yeah, but it won't be easy." Caleb surveyed the steep slope. "It's straight uphill."

"Great," she said, tightening her grip on her bow. "Lead the way."

"Why do you want to go there?" he asked. "The tunnels aren't there anymore."

"Maybe we'll find one that didn't collapse."

"I highly doubt it."

Adeline shot him a harsh, disapproving look.

"I'm just stating the obvious," he said, raising his hands.

"We'll be fine."

"Whatever." Caleb stepped off the path, forcing his way through the trees. Adeline followed close behind, pushing aside branches as weeds scraped her shins, leaving them itchy. The climb was brutal, steeper and more exhausting than she'd expected. And it only got worse. Sweat soaked her clothes as she pressed on. Her calves burned with each stride. The uphill trek forced her to scramble over boulders and weave through briars and thick brush.

Adeline slowed her pace, her breath coming in shallow gasps. "Hold up. I need a break."

"Me too," Caleb panted, wiping his face with the hem of his shirt.

Leaning her bow against a tree, Adeline took a few deep breaths. Her head was spinning, and her mouth felt like sandpaper. They needed water—soon.

She glanced over at Caleb and stilled. He was staring at her, his face devoid of emotion.

Insecurity crept in, and she quickly looked away. She didn't need a mirror to know she looked awful.

"How old are you?" Caleb asked, sweat trickling down his neck.

"How old do you think I am?"

"Twelve."

Adeline fired him a look. "How'd you know?"

"Your immaturity gave it away."

"You're one to talk."

His gaze didn't waver. "Seriously, how old are you?"

"Seventeen," she said, grabbing her bow. "Do you know if there's any water nearby?"

"There's a water pump at the mine," he said. "Not sure if it still works."

"Let's hope it does."

Caleb said nothing, but the look on his face said enough as he kept climbing. Adeline followed, praying he was wrong.

They hiked at a slow pace, but Adeline struggled to keep up. Every step was a battle, her muscles trembling with fatigue. She grabbed a tree for support, panting as sweat poured down her face. Her legs wobbled beneath her.

She forced a few more steps before stopping. "I can't go any further."

"We're almost there." Caleb was breathing hard, his hands on his hips.

"I can't," she said, dropping her bow. She pressed her palm against a tree, trying to steady herself, but a wave of dizziness swept over her. The forest tilted. Her knees buckled. She closed her eyes as everything spun and fell backward.

Firm hands caught her and eased her to the ground.

"Adeline!" Caleb tapped her cheek. "Can you hear me?"

Adeline slowly opened her eyes to find Caleb hovering over her.

"You okay?"

She blinked up at him, her head swimming. A few seconds passed before she could sit up. Leaves clung to her back as she rubbed her pounding forehead.

"You need water," Caleb said, standing. He glanced up the mountain. "Can you stand?"

Adeline gave a weak shake of her head, too exhausted to reply.

"You have to." Caleb grabbed her wrists and pulled her up. "We can't stay here."

Adeline rose on shaky legs but lost all strength. She collapsed forward, crashing into Caleb's chest.

Curses spewed from Caleb as he caught her, stumbling back a step. He steadied her with his hands on her hips. "We have to keep moving."

His nearness should've made her uncomfortable, but she was past the point of caring. Slowly, she lifted her head until their eyes met. His irises were captivating up close, mostly green with a touch of gold, but the lack of compassion in them repelled her. All she saw was frustration.

"I need a break," she muttered, looking away.

"You can take a break when we get to the mine." Caleb looped her arm around his thin shoulders, then wrapped his own around her back, gripping her waist. Once steady, he bent to pick up her bow and started the climb.

"Why are you helping me?" she asked, her legs dragging with each step.

"You're my only way out of this place." His fingers bit into her side, urging her forward.

The hike was slow and grueling. Adeline kept tripping over roots and rocks, but Caleb held her up. Together, they pushed upward until they reached the mine.

Chapter Eighteen

The old mine was nothing more than a decaying settlement littered with junk and crumbling buildings. Scrap metal and rusted debris lay scattered, overtaken by weeds that choked the area.

It was quiet and appeared to be deserted. At least Adeline hoped it was as Caleb helped her hobble toward a rusted water pump standing alone in the sunlit clearing.

Once they reached it, Caleb steadied her. "I'll see if it works," he said, giving the area a quick sweep. "Can you stand by yourself?"

"I think so." Adeline slipped her sweaty arm from his shoulder. Her head was still pounding, but she felt steady enough to stand on her own.

"You good?"

She gave a small nod, and he slowly let go of her waist. Setting the bow beside her, he stepped up to the pump and gripped the rusted handle. It let out a grating screech as he moved the handle up and down.

No water.

He pumped harder, his thin muscles flexing with each jerk.

All at once, a rush of water spewed from the pump, splashing onto the ground.

Caleb's face lit up with joy. "It works!"

He took a long drink before shoving his entire head under the stream. Water went everywhere, soaking his dreadlocks and clothes, but he didn't seem to care. His genuine smile never left as he scrubbed the grime from his face.

Adeline watched, a grin pulling on her own lips. She'd never seen him happy before.

Why can't he always be like this?

The stream slowed, and Caleb went back to pumping. Another burst of water flowed out.

"My turn." Adeline staggered to the pump and leaned in, sticking her mouth beneath the water. She closed her eyes as she took a long sip, gripping the top of the pump to steady herself. The water was ice-cold and felt incredible sliding down her parched throat.

Caleb kept the handle moving so she could drink more. Once she'd had enough, she cupped her hands and splashed water onto her grimy face. It stole her breath and sent a shiver racing down her spine. As she wiped the droplets from her eyes, the icy rush left her feeling instantly refreshed.

Before she could get another handful of water, Caleb barged in, bumping her to the side. He took a quick sip before scrubbing the filth off his arms and neck.

Adeline couldn't take her eyes off him as she pumped more water for him. His expression stayed light and carefree as he laughed softly, splashing more water over his dirty skin. There was something about his smile that transformed his whole face. Despite needing a serious cleaning, his straight teeth and unguarded joy seemed to erase the pain and anger that usually defined his face.

"Told you he wasn't all bad." Jesse's voice entered her thoughts.

"He's tolerable," she said, fighting a grin.

"Give him time. You won't believe how much he changes."

"I'll believe it when I see it." She released the handle. *"But enough about Caleb. How do we get to the cabin from here?"*

"The building closest to the mine has the answers you're looking for."

"Meaning?"

"Go see for yourself."

Not wanting to waste time, Adeline stepped away from the pump. She held back a groan as she grabbed her bow and looped it over her shoulder. Now that she felt better, she took a closer look at the area.

Thick forest surrounded the small settlement that had seen better days. Vines climbed the brick walls of the abandoned houses, threading through broken windows and open doorways. Some homes had been swallowed entirely by nature. She finally spotted the brick house Jesse had mentioned. Though it was just as old as the other buildings, it appeared to be in better shape.

"I can't believe that old pump still works." Caleb wrung out his knotted hair as he approached Adeline.

"I know. We'd have been in trouble if it didn't."

"No kidding."

"Come on. Let's check out that building," she said, pointing to the one closest to the mine.

"I thought we were heading into the mine."

"Not yet," she said, pushing through the weeds. "We need to go there first."

Caleb caught up to her. "Why?"

"Jesse told me to."

Caleb grabbed her bicep, stopping her. "Jesse isn't here."

She pulled her arm free. "I already told you. I can talk to him in my head."

Water dripped down Caleb's face as he studied her, his expression impossible to read. She waited for him to ridicule her, to challenge her. Instead, he took a step back. "Okay."

"Wow." She tilted her head, surprised. "No rude comments?"

"Don't push your luck."

Adeline hid a grin as she passed the dilapidated buildings, heading straight to the brick house near the mine. Ivy smothered most of the one-story structure, while weeds and overgrown bushes crowded the front entrance.

Her legs itched as she pushed through the tall, scratchy weeds with Caleb close behind her. Reaching the porch, they hesitated, pressing their weight into the weathered boards before moving toward the door plagued by vines. Adeline used her hands to tear them away until she uncovered the doorknob. It twisted, but the door wouldn't open.

"It's stuck," she said, giving it a shove.

"Let me try."

Caleb pushed Adeline aside and grabbed the doorknob. He rammed his shoulder into the door; it burst open with a loud creak.

Sunlight poured into the room, revealing a living area in disarray. Cobwebs draped the sagging furniture, and dust coated every surface, including the outdated fireplace. The floor was littered with trash and forgotten junk. No one had been there in ages.

A stagnant smell greeted Adeline as she stepped inside. She picked up an old candleholder from the floor and blew off the dust. "I wonder who lived here."

"Probably one of the miners." Caleb walked up beside her. "What exactly are we looking for?"

"Not sure." She set the candleholder on the end table. "Jesse told me the answers we need are in here."

"Right," Caleb said before walking into the adjacent room.

Adeline went the other way, entering a small bedroom with a rusted metal bedframe and a mold-covered mattress. There was nothing there but old clothes and mounds of dust.

Wiping her dirty hands on her jean shorts, she left the room and found Caleb in the kitchen. "Did you find anything?" she asked, approaching from behind.

"Nope." He shut a cabinet with a soft thud. "Nothing here but expired food and trash."

"I'll check the last room."

"I'll go with you."

The final room was an office and just as messy as the rest. Papers and trash covered the floor and cluttered the old oak desk that stood in front of a massive bookshelf. The shelves stretched across the back wall, packed with books from end to end. Adeline headed straight for the desk while Caleb wandered over to the books.

Sifting through the dusty piles of letters, Adeline found nothing interesting. Most were old reports from when the mine was active. The stale air gave her a headache as she opened the top drawer and pulled out another stack of papers. She skimmed through each one. Nothing important.

Just as she went to close the drawer, something tucked in the back corner caught her eye. It was a crumpled sheet of paper. She reached for it and carefully placed it on the desk, smoothing it out with her hands. She leaned in, her pulse quickening with anticipation as her eyes raced over it. A spark of hope surged through her.

"I found a map!" she said, holding it up.

"A map of what?"

"The mine."

Caleb snatched it from her and gave it a quick scan. "It's not a map of the mine."

"How do you know?" she asked, grabbing it back.

"The mine up here only had two tunnels," he said. "That map has at least twenty."

Caleb returned to the bookshelf while Adeline examined the faded paper. The intricate details convinced her it *had* to be the right map. Caleb might know the area better than she did, but she had to trust her instincts.

It won't hurt to keep it. She folded the map and slipped it into her back pocket.

Leaning back against the desk, Adeline watched as Caleb pulled books from the shelf. He opened each one for a quick peek before tossing it aside. Each landed with a thud, sending up a fresh billow of dust.

"Find anything?" she asked.

"It'd help if I knew what we were looking for," Caleb said, dropping another book to the floor.

Adeline exhaled hard, frustration bubbling to the surface. *"Why are we here, Jesse?"*

"Keep looking."

Adeline crossed her arms as Caleb tore through the remaining shelves. Half of the books were already on the floor. It wouldn't take him long to go through the rest.

Caleb reached for another book but had trouble pulling it free from the shelf. It acted as if it was glued in place. "This one's stuck," he said without looking back.

"That's strange." Adeline pushed off the desk. "Try pressing it."

Caleb pressed the spine.

Click.

The book sank inward, and the bookshelf popped open on the left side. It was a secret door.

Eyes wide, Caleb approached the narrow opening and tugged the bookshelf toward him. It squeaked as it widened.

"What is it?" Adeline asked, standing behind him.

"I can't see anything." Caleb stuck his head inside. "It's too dark."

Adeline helped pull the door out even more. Light streamed into the secret passageway, revealing what looked like the entrance to a cave. Everything was rock, including the long flight of steps that went down into darkness. Her mouth went dry as she stared at the eerie steps. "I wonder where it goes."

"Not anywhere we want to go."

Pulling her glass dagger from its sheath, Adeline tapped it twice against her palm until it lit up. Jesse had taught her that trick a while back.

"It lights up too?" Caleb asked, the light illuminating his confused face.

"Yeah." Adeline raised the dagger high, casting a bright light around them. "I think this is what Jesse wanted us to find. It must be a way through the mountain."

"We can't go in there." Caleb blocked the entrance with his body. "For all we know, it could lead us right to Ralock."

"Move, Caleb."

He didn't budge. "I don't think it's smart to follow a hidden staircase we found behind a bookshelf."

"We're going down those steps," she said, her voice stern.

"*No*, we're not. We don't know where they go."

"Fine. Stay here. I don't care." Her eyes burned into his. "But I'm going in there."

A hard look tightened his features as his jaw flexed. "Your ignorance will get us killed."

"My so-called *ignorance* got us this far. This is your last chance, Caleb. Are you coming with me or not?"

He looked away, his lips pressing into a thin line. After a pause, he stepped to the side, gesturing to the entrance. "Lead the way, princess."

Adeline glared at him. She wanted to slap him, but doing so would only make things worse.

Letting it go, she proceeded to the stairway.

Moments like this made Adeline question why she was even helping Caleb. He wasn't just ungrateful. He argued about everything.

Why is it so hard for him to be nice?

Shaking off her annoyance, Adeline lifted her glowing blade. The light reflected off the stone walls, revealing a long, narrow staircase that vanished into blackness.

Goosebumps raced across her skin as she started down. Maybe it was the cold. Maybe fear. Either way, she hoped the tunnel was their way out.

Chapter Nineteen

Adeline and Caleb snuck down the stairway, their sneakers slapping softly against the stone steps. Caleb hadn't uttered a word since they'd started, but he stayed close since her dagger was their only source of light.

The stairway didn't seem to have an end. Each step led to more steps. Adeline wondered if they'd ever reach the bottom.

Slam!

Adeline froze, her heart launching into her throat. "Was that the secret door?"

"I hope not," Caleb said, his voice tight with fear.

A deafening silence stretched, broken only by their uneven breaths. A full minute passed.

"I'm going to take a look," she said quietly.

"I'm coming with you."

Adeline's calves burned as they climbed, their footfalls echoing eerily in the stillness. When they reached the top, Adeline stopped cold.

The door was gone. It had sealed itself into the rock as if it had never existed.

"This is not good," Adeline said, working to stay calm.

Caleb stormed past her and slammed both hands against the cave wall. Nothing happened. He screamed in rage, his fist striking the rough rock. The door stayed sealed.

"There's got to be a lever or something to open it," Adeline said, waving her glowing weapon across the walls.

The flickering light threw distorted shadows over the rocks as she searched for anything unusual. There wasn't a button, a lever, or anything she could find to open the door.

"Well, isn't this just great?" Caleb kicked the closed entrance. "Your brilliant idea got us locked inside a cave."

"You didn't have to come with me."

"I wish I hadn't!"

"Yelling at me won't change anything, so *shut up*!"

Caleb clenched his fists, his breaths growing faster as he glared at her. He looked like he was about to punch her. Part of her hoped he would. It would give her an excuse to hit him back.

But to her disappointment, he did nothing.

With a final sneer, Adeline spun on her heels and went deeper into the unknown. Caleb had no choice but to follow.

Down the stairs they went, neither saying a word. Adeline trembled as they descended, trying not to think about their dilemma. Hopefully, they'd find a way out.

The hair on the back of her neck stood up as they reached the bottom. She stopped and held her dagger high.

Busted bottles, broken boxes, and scrap metal lined the sides of the creepy tunnel. A narrow path ran straight down the middle. It was clear enough for them to walk without issue. Among the rubble, an old lantern stood out to Adeline. With her bow still resting on her shoulder, she reached for it. Rust and grime coated the metal frame, but to her surprise, there was still oil inside it.

"Do you have any matches?" she asked, turning to face Caleb.

He gave her an annoyed look. "Do I look like I would have matches?"

"I was just asking."

Adeline exhaled in frustration and turned back to the pile of junk, looking for anything that might light the lamp. The lantern wasn't essential. They had her dagger. But it would make things easier.

"Use your dagger to light the wick." Henry's familiar accent bounced around her mind.

"My dagger?"

"Yes. Hold the blade to the wick and see what happens."

It sounded ridiculous, but she decided to try it. What was the worst that could happen?

The moment her dagger touched the old wick, it crackled.

Adeline jerked back as light burst from the lantern as if she had lit a firework. A steady flame remained, casting a warm orange glow along the stone walls.

"How did you do that?" Caleb asked, rushing to her side.

"Apparently, my dagger can also be used as a lighter."

"And you knew this...how?"

"Henry told me." She shoved the lantern into his chest. "Let's go."

Caleb mumbled something under his breath, but Adeline ignored him as she headed down the eerie passageway. Their feet tapped against the rocky floor as they walked, Caleb trailing behind her.

Light poured ahead, revealing a small doorway cut into the wall. It was barely visible, especially with the heap of junk piled at the entrance.

The main tunnel continued, but Adeline paused when she reached the opening. She kicked the trash away and peeked inside, her light spilling down another passageway. It was longer than the light could reach.

"Let's go this way," she said, staring inside the new tunnel.

"That's a good way to get lost."

"We're not going to get lost."

"Says the girl who got us locked inside a bookshelf."

Adeline jabbed the tip of her dagger into his chest. "Is it really that hard for you to keep your mouth shut?"

Caleb dipped his eyes to the blade, then back to her. "What are you going to do? Stab me?"

"Don't push me." She lowered her weapon and stepped into the newly discovered passage.

Irritation and fear roiled within her as she pushed forward, Caleb reluctantly following.

I hope this is the way out.

After walking twenty paces, a staircase appeared. It looked exactly like the one they'd used earlier.

"Stay here," Adeline said, placing a foot on the first step.

"I'm not staying here by myself."

"All right."

Adeline led the way up the stairway. Each step pulled at her aching muscles, but she didn't stop. When she reached the top, her heart plummeted.

A dead end.

Sighing, she slipped the bow from her sore shoulder and sank onto the top step. The fiery ache in her legs matched the chaos in her mind as she laid her weapons beside her and tried to catch her breath. "There has to be a way out."

Caleb dropped beside her, breathing just as hard. "I wish we had a map or something."

"The map!" Adeline popped to her feet.

Caleb frowned as she pulled a folded paper from her back pocket. Her hands shook as she unfolded it, the paper crackling in the quiet. One glance, and her breath hitched.

"You were right, Caleb." She dropped back down beside him, scanning the many short tunnels drawn across the page. "This isn't a map of the mine; it's a map of this tunnel!"

Caleb snatched it from her hands, his face lighting up. "You're right." He let out a quick laugh. "I can't believe it. What made you keep it?"

"I thought it was the mine map," she said, tugging it back.

"So you didn't believe me?"

"Exactly," she said, her grin playful.

Caleb moved the lantern closer and pointed. "This one here. It looks like it leads outside."

"You think that's our way out?"

"It has to be."

"Then let's find it." Adeline rose, stretching her stiff limbs. "Here, take the map. You can read it better than I can."

"You're trusting me to lead the way?" Caleb asked, rising to his feet as he took the paper.

"I am." She shouldered her bow and picked up her glowing dagger. "So don't screw it up."

"Yes, ma'am."

Chapter Twenty

The pressure in Adeline's chest eased slightly now that they had an outline of the tunnel. She was still on edge, but it wasn't as suffocating as before.

Light skimmed across the tunnel walls as they moved together through the trash and junk that littered the sides. The farther they went, the more Adeline realized just how huge the tunnel really was. Countless passageways branched off on both sides. Without the map, they would've been in serious trouble.

Caleb navigated with confidence until the tunnel split into multiple passageways. There were five in total, all identical. He chewed his bottom lip, his eyes flicking between the map and the tunnels.

Worry crept over Adeline as she adjusted her bow on her shoulder. He was taking longer than usual.

Caleb pointed to the far-left tunnel. "It's that one."

"Are you sure?"

"Positive." He glanced once more at the map, then stepped toward the tunnel.

"I hope you're right."

Adeline followed, doubt lingering in the back of her mind. The tunnel was far messier than the others. Trash and metal scraps spilled onto the walkway, threatening to trip Caleb as he kept his nose buried in the map.

A large, dark shape materialized ahead. Something about it felt off. Adeline skidded to a stop and grabbed Caleb's shirt, yanking him backward.

"What?" He looked up, startled.

Adeline pointed. "What is that?"

Caleb squinted as he raised the lantern. "It's probably just trash."

"Stay back. I'll take a look." Adeline snuck forward, her grip tightening on her blade. Light stretched toward the shape and then revealed it.

Adeline froze, chills blasting down her back.

Three skeletons were piled atop one another, their shredded clothes and rotting boots still clinging to the bone.

"What is it?" Caleb called from behind her.

"It's definitely not trash," she said, her chest tight with fear as she stepped closer to the skeletons. Their hollow eyes seemed to mock her as she stood over them.

Caleb joined her. "Maybe they got lost."

"Or maybe someone murdered them."

Adeline crouched and pulled a sword from a ribcage. The jagged black blade made her shiver as she lifted it to the light. It was even more disturbing up close, identical to the weapons she'd seen in that cursed territory.

A sudden warmth traveled up her arm, as if she'd received an injection. It was strange, but not unpleasant. The heat spread through her body, awakening something inside her. With each passing second, she felt stronger. Unstoppable.

Alarm bells screamed in her head. She dropped the sword and took a step back.

Something about that weapon wasn't right.

Unease coiled in her chest as Caleb set the lantern down and scooped up the blade. He smirked, examining the sharp edge before giving it a casual swing.

Dread swept over her as she eyed the black blade. It looked like the one he'd wielded before. The one he'd tried to kill her with.

"You should put it back," she said.

"I need a weapon." Caleb's gaze hardened.

"We'll find you a different one."

"These are the only weapons allowed in this territory." He held it up. "All others are forbidden."

Adeline studied the ominous blade, her stomach twisting. It would be safer if they both had weapons. Maybe she was just overreacting.

"Fine," she said, picking up the lantern Caleb had abandoned. "Keep it."

Caleb stepped around the skeletons, the map in one hand and the sword in the other. Adeline followed closely behind, both lights casting long shadows down the cluttered tunnel. There wasn't an end, just darkness pressing in around them.

Caleb glanced at the map now and then, but most of his focus was on the blade. He swung it around like a kid with a new toy. They passed several side tunnels, but he didn't seem to notice. He was too fixated on the weapon to notice anything else.

Adeline's stomach twisted. He wasn't just distracted; he was enjoying that sword.

"Are we getting close?" she asked.

Caleb cast her a dark look. "What do I look like? Your tour guide?"

Adeline pressed her lips together, holding back her wrath. The temptation to hit him flared again. With a huff, she turned off the light on her dagger, stashed it, and snatched the map from his hand. She held the lantern above the page, its steady glow illuminating the worn paper.

It took her a minute to figure out where they were. Once she did, hope ignited in her. They were close to the exit.

Adeline shook off her irritation and kept walking. Caleb trailed behind, matching her pace as she lifted the lantern higher to avoid tripping.

Ten minutes passed, and a hole in the rock wall appeared. It was a few feet off the ground and looked to be the size of a window.

That must be it.

Her heart rate quickened as she stepped closer and peered inside. She couldn't see where it led.

Tucking the map into her back pocket, she gripped the rough rock and carefully climbed through, doing her best not to drop the lantern. A chill spread down her arms as she raised the light.

The flame peeled back the darkness, revealing another tunnel occupied by spiderwebs and dust. Unlike the others, there was no trash. Just an unsettling silence, like the place had been untouched for decades.

Adeline shivered as she looked ahead.

There, at the end of the tunnel, was a faint light.

A grin spread across her face. *The exit.*

Chapter Twenty-One

"I see light!" Adeline said, her heart soaring.

Caleb scrambled through the hole, black sword in hand. He marched toward the exit, completely ignoring her. The lack of light didn't seem to faze him. When had he gotten so brave?

Adeline had to power walk to keep up with his long strides. He sliced through the spiderwebs with his blade, never glancing back as he forged ahead like a man on a mission. His loud footsteps echoed in her ears as delicate strands of web brushed her skin.

She couldn't understand his sudden urgency. Was he sick of the tunnel? Or maybe he just really needed some fresh air.

Dust caked Adeline's sneakers by the time they neared the exit. Long, vibrant vines hung over the opening like party decor, intertwined with tree branches that concealed the secret tunnel. A sliver of sunlight managed to break through the thick vegetation.

Caleb hacked away at the overgrowth, sending tree limbs and vines tumbling onto his shoes. He didn't stop until sunlight poured into the tunnel.

Adeline raised a hand to shield her eyes from the sudden brightness as a warm breeze swept in. An earthy aroma, heavy with pine, filled her lungs.

Excitement and caution stirred in her as she blew out the lantern, leaving it behind as she stepped outside with Caleb. The sun's rays tickled her cheeks as she breathed in the fresh air. It felt amazing to be outside again.

They were deep in a dense forest, with no sign of life anywhere. The trees rocked gently in the unseen wind, their leaves brushing together in near silence.

The usual hum of the woods was missing. No birds. No insects. Just an eerie hush that clung to everything.

"Do you know where we are?" she asked. They had to be on the other side of the mountain.

"How would I know?" Caleb said coldly.

Annoyance flattened her lips. "I was just wondering. You don't need to get all mad."

Caleb rolled his eyes and started down the mountain. There wasn't a trail, so he made his own through the thick forest.

Adeline followed, scanning the area for Ralock and his hunters. If any of them were nearby, they'd definitely hear Caleb. Dry sticks cracked under his feet as he hacked through plants and low-hanging branches. It was as though he no longer cared about getting caught.

After five solid minutes of trying to keep up, Adeline stopped. "I think we should figure out where we are."

Caleb turned to her with an unsettling expression. Smoke seemed to cloud his golden-green eyes, making them look hazy. "Who made you the boss?"

"What's your problem?" Adeline clenched her fists, her nails digging into her palms. "I'm trying to get us out of here."

"Find your own way out." Caleb started hiking again. "I don't need you."

"Caleb!" she yelled as he widened the gap between them. "We have to stay together!"

He ignored her and kept walking away.

Adeline's patience evaporated. She loaded her bow, aiming it at Caleb. For a second, she thought about nicking his shoulder, but decided against it. Her plan was to get his attention, not harm him.

Zing!

The arrow flew past Caleb, striking a nearby tree. He glared at the wobbling shaft, teeth clenched.

"Next time I won't miss," Adeline warned. "Now come back here."

Anger knitted Caleb's brows together as he chopped the arrow in half and fired Adeline a nasty look. She instinctively took a step back, her throat locking tight. The emptiness in his gaze was exactly like the day she'd met him. He wanted to hurt her.

Caleb whipped back his arm and hurled the sword at her. The blade flipped in the air like a boomerang, spinning straight toward her chest.

Adeline leaped out of the way just before the sword plowed into a tree.

Fear rattled in her chest as she stared at the swaying blade. *He could've killed me.*

Pounding footsteps reached her ears. She had barely turned before Caleb barreled into her. He tackled her to the ground, knocking her bow from her hand. Pain seared up her back as she wheezed for air, struggling to free herself beneath Caleb. She bucked and twisted, but she was no match for his unexpected strength as he straddled her.

Hatred blazed in his eyes as he pulled back his fist and punched her.

Adeline's head snapped back as pain exploded in her cheek. Her vision blurred, and a heavy fog weighed down her eyelids. She fought to stay conscious.

Caleb sprang off her and went to retrieve his sword from the thick hickory tree. He tugged hard on the handle, but it wouldn't come loose.

Adeline rolled onto her side, pressing her palms to the earth. Her head throbbed as she lifted herself and leaned against a tree. Everything was spinning as she zeroed in on Caleb, who was still fighting to free his sword. He had his back to her, cursing with both hands on the hilt and one foot braced against the tree. He'd thrown that blade harder than she'd realized.

Adeline watched him struggle, her lips pinching tight. He would pay for hitting her.

The throbbing in her head and cheek dulled as anger and adrenaline took over. Her hand shook as she unsheathed her dagger, the glass blade rasping against the jeweled sheath.

At that very moment, Caleb yanked the sword from the tree. He rocked back a step, then steadied himself before turning to Adeline. "You should've killed me when you had the chance."

The darkness in his tone made her hair stand on end. She was still furious at him, but now she saw it clearly. He wasn't in his right mind.

What do I do?

Caleb was stomping toward her, and she had seconds to decide. She didn't want to hurt him, but doing nothing wasn't an option.

A fierce growl rumbled from his throat as he swung the sword at her head.

Adeline ducked, the black steel missing her ear by an inch. "What's wrong with you?"

Caleb roared as he came at her even harder.

She jumped back, avoiding the blade. "Stop, Caleb!"

Her mind raced as she backed away. She was a better fighter; maybe she could knock him out. It seemed like a good idea, but she couldn't carry or drag him to the cabin. Plus, she didn't even know where they were.

"Destroying the sword will break the demonic power over Caleb." Henry's accent filled her mind.

Of course! Her frantic thoughts calmed. *It's the sword that's making him crazy.*

A new confidence rose now that she had a solid plan. She'd destroyed his sword once. She could do it again.

Pure evil burned in Caleb's eyes as he charged at her. When he got close, he slashed at her chest.

Adeline sprang back, nearly colliding with a tree. There was only a fleeting moment before Caleb attacked again. She ducked just as his blade hit the tree trunk, showering her with bark, then scrambled over the raised roots to get into a better position.

Time and again, Adeline dodged his advances, waiting for the perfect moment to strike.

Then it came.

With a cry, Adeline swung her dagger with everything she had.

Crack!

Her blade pulverized his sword like brittle glass. Black fragments scattered across the forest floor as Caleb stumbled back. Miraculously, none of the sharp shards struck either of them.

A terrifying noise tore from Caleb's throat as his eyes remained fixed on the broken weapon. He kept his head down, staring at the black shards that littered the ground. His breathing was rough as he dropped the broken handle.

Adeline took a cautious step forward. "Caleb?"

He looked at her, and his frown deepened. The cloudiness in his eyes had vanished, replaced by remorse. He backed up, raising a hand to ward her off. "You need to get away from me. I'm dangerous."

"No, you're not." Adeline stashed her weapon. "That wicked sword made you act all crazy."

"I'm sorry," he said while rubbing his forehead with shaking fingers. "I shouldn't have picked it up."

"I'll forgive you this time." Adeline forced a small smile as she touched her bruised cheek. "Besides, I barely felt it."

His lips quirked upward but quickly returned to a frown. He clearly didn't believe her.

"Do you have any idea where we are?" she asked, a headache returning as she scanned the thick forest. Her face was throbbing now that her adrenaline had worn off. At least he had missed her eye.

Caleb slowly shook his head. "Not at the moment."

A sudden groan escaped him, and he collapsed to his knees as if he'd been struck. He clutched his head, his eyes screwed shut.

"Caleb!" Adeline rushed forward. "What's wrong?"

For a long second, he didn't respond. Then his eyes snapped open.

Launching to his feet, Caleb snatched Adeline's bow off the ground before grabbing her wrist and pulling her through the trees.

"What are you doing?" she cried, trying to pull free. "Let go of me!"

Branches whipped at her arms and face as Caleb dragged her behind him, his grip tightening with every step.

"They're coming for me," he said, not slowing down.

Adeline tripped over a root but managed to stay upright. "What are you talking about?"

Caleb skidded to a halt by a large tree and freed her wrist. He gave it a thorough look before turning to her, his face pale with fear. "Ralock and his hunters will be here any minute. You need to hide."

"What?" She searched his worried face for answers. "How do you know that?"

"I just had a vision."

Horror tightened her throat. He was telling the truth.

Caleb shoved aside the overgrown plants, revealing a hollow section in the base of the tree. He stuffed her bow inside, grabbed her hand, and pulled her toward the opening. "Hide in there, and do *not* come out."

"I'm not leaving you. They'll kill you."

Caleb placed his trembling hands on her shoulders, locking eyes with her. "Get in that tree, Adeline."

Something in his tone chilled her to the bone. He wanted to protect her. But what about him?

She wanted to argue, to fight back. But her gut told her not to. She needed to hide.

Weeds scraped her legs as she removed her quiver and climbed into the hollowed tree. Pressing back against the trunk, Adeline slid down into the dirt and pulled her knees to her chest. The space was tight, but she could sit comfortably with her bow propped up at her feet.

Fast-approaching footsteps sounded in the distance.

Caleb scrambled to rearrange the bushes and shrubs, concealing her hiding place. He glanced over his shoulder, then back at the tree. Adeline could partially see him through the leaves. "Stay there," he whispered.

Shouting pierced the air. They were close.

Caleb bolted in the opposite direction, his sneakers pounding into the forest floor as he pumped his arms.

A rock the size of a baseball whizzed through the trees, nailing Caleb in the back. He hit the dirt face-first, groaning. He'd only made it a few yards.

Adeline started to climb out of her hiding spot. She had to help him.

"Stay where you are," Henry's voice echoed inside her head.

"Ralock will kill him!"

"He'll kill you too if he sees you."

Moisture filled her eyes as she watched Caleb through the leaves. He held his back as he slowly rose to his feet.

Moments later, Ralock emerged with a group of hunters. There were at least ten of them, each wielding a black-bladed sword.

Fear flooded Adeline's veins. Caleb didn't stand a chance.

"After everything I've done for you," Ralock said, wearing the same three-piece suit as before. "You still run from me."

Caleb stared at the ground, silent.

"Where's your little friend?" Ralock glanced around. "I thought for sure she'd be with you."

"She isn't here," Caleb said in almost a whisper.

Smack!

Ralock slapped Caleb hard across the face, nearly knocking him to the ground. He stayed upright, shaking as he cradled his reddening cheek.

"Find her," Ralock ordered, turning to his hunters.

Adeline clapped a hand over her mouth, her heart hammering, as the hunters split up to search for her. Leaves and sticks crunched under their combat boots as they spread through the forest, searching high and low.

"I know you're lying." Ralock snatched Caleb's chin, forcing him to meet his gaze. "It's written all over your face."

Caleb said nothing, his face losing all color.

"Where is she?"

"I swear I don't know!" Caleb shouted as blood dripped off his face.

"There's no point in helping her," Ralock said, releasing him with a shove. "She wouldn't do it for you."

Caleb held his chin, crimson staining his trembling fingers. He looked like he might collapse.

One of the hunters approached Ralock with a black sword in hand. He leaned in close, whispering so only Ralock could hear.

Adeline's stomach did a somersault when Caleb glanced in her direction. He couldn't possibly see her through the brush, but he must've known she was watching him. With the faintest shake of his head, he warned her not to reveal herself. Not to fight for him.

Tears blurred her vision. When had Caleb become so heroic? He could have easily hidden himself.

Why did he choose to protect me?

Silent tears streamed down her cheeks as the hunters continued their search. They passed her hideout multiple times but never looked twice. Caleb must've done a good job concealing it.

After what felt like forever, one hunter marched up to Ralock. "She isn't here, Master."

Ralock's jaw tightened. "Assemble the others and find her. She shouldn't be far. And blow up the tunnel entrance, just in case she's hiding in there."

A group of hunters headed toward the mountain while Ralock stayed with Caleb. He looked helpless with his head hung low, his eyes cast downward.

Hopelessness weaved through Adeline. She wanted to save Caleb. To rescue him from Ralock. To do something. But she stayed put as fresh tears fell.

BANG!

Adeline's body jerked as a loud explosion rocked the air, terror spiking through her.

"As for you, my little runaway..." Ralock reached over his head, grabbing the sword on his back. "You're coming with me."

He crashed the metal handle into Caleb's forehead, knocking him down. Blood poured down his face as he lay sprawled out. He was out cold.

No! Adeline held back a scream.

Ralock grabbed a fistful of Caleb's dreadlocks and dragged him away. Caleb's limp body scraped across the forest floor, collecting sticks and dirt. It took only a moment until they disappeared from view.

Adeline squeezed her eyes shut against more tears. *I'll never see him again.*

Silence struck the forest, and Adeline couldn't hold in her emotions anymore. She sobbed, covering her mouth with her hand.

She didn't stop crying until the sun began to set. Her throat was raw and her mind numb as the forest darkened. Cramps seized her body, and the pressure in her head became unbearable. Part of her longed to flee to the cabin, to escape it all, but she wouldn't make it far. Exhaustion was closing in. She needed to rest.

Leaning her head back against the trunk, Adeline let her heavy eyes close and fell into a deep sleep.

Chapter Twenty-Two

Slivers of light slipped into Adeline's hiding place as she stirred awake. Rubbing the sleep from her eyes, she groaned as she shifted her stiff, aching body. She had to get out of that tree.

She reached for the edge of the opening but froze when she heard the faint crackle of a nearby campfire.

Sweat prickled her hairline as she peered through the leafy branches. A tall, fit man stood before a small fire, his back to her. Blood and sweat stained his torn, dirty clothes. Even without seeing his face, she knew exactly who he was.

Jesse.

Adeline scurried out of her hiding spot, wild with relief as she crashed into Jesse's open arms. She squeezed him tightly, unable to stop the flow of tears. "I was so afraid," she said, her voice breaking.

"I know."

Jesse rested his chin gently on top of her head as he held her in place, his filthy T-shirt soaking up her tears. He smelled of sweat and smoke, but she didn't care. For the first time in days, peace settled over her.

Adeline stepped back and wiped her eyes. "Are you all right?"

Red dust from the desert clung to Jesse's messy bun and beard. It was even on his tan skin and the scrapes along his arms. Overall, he looked okay. Minus the dark circles under his eyes. He clearly hadn't slept in a while.

"Of course." Jesse gave a weary smile. "Those warriors didn't stand a chance."

"Did you kill them all?"

"Yep. They won't be bothering Blistering Heights anymore."

"That's good," she said, relieved he wasn't hurt. "How'd you get here?"

"I borrowed a horse."

Adeline skimmed the quiet forest. "Where is it?"

"I sent it home before I reached the boundary line," Jesse said, brushing a finger gently across her swollen cheek. "Nice bruise you've got there."

Adeline flinched as the pain reawakened. "I should thank Caleb for that one."

"It makes you look tough."

Cracking a smile, she ran her fingers over the bruise before lightly touching the lump on her forehead. She could only imagine how awful she looked. "Ralock captured Caleb," she said, letting her hand fall to her side.

"That's why I'm here."

"Is he dead?" she asked, her voice choked with emotion.

"No." Jesse shook his head. "He's locked up in the barracks."

Relief hit her first, only to be swallowed by a rush of fear. "What are they going to do to him?"

"Nothing more if we get to him in time."

A look of disbelief crossed her face. "You think we can save him?"

"Of course we can."

"How?"

"You don't need to know the details." He sat by the fire. "Just know that we're going to rescue *our* friend."

Our friend.

A couple of days ago, Adeline would never have considered Caleb a friend. But after he'd risked his life for hers, her perspective had changed.

"Sit," Jesse said, gesturing toward the campfire.

Adeline lowered herself across from him, her leg muscles aching as she crossed them.

"Here." Jesse tossed her a water tin.

She caught it midair and took a long gulp. The water soothed her dry throat as she took another sip, some spilling down her chin.

"Thanks." She wiped her mouth with the back of her hand. "Do you have any food? I'm starving."

"I sure do," he said, sliding his backpack around the fire. "You can have whatever you want."

Adeline tore through the bag, her stomach growling as she uncovered the stash of food. Dried fruit. Beef jerky. Granola bars. And more. The options were endless.

For the next few minutes, she stuffed her mouth with whatever she could grab.

"Someone was hungry," Jesse said, his lips quirking upward.

"You have no idea," she said, tossing another handful of trail mix into her mouth.

Adeline ate until she was stuffed, then leaned back against a tree. The flames calmed her weary mind. Her head still pounded and her body ached, but at least she wasn't hungry.

"How did Ralock find us?" she asked, tossing a wrapper into the fire.

"He was tracking Caleb."

Her brows pinched together. "How?"

"The cobra tattoo on his arm is a tracking device," Jesse said, taking a sip of water.

"What?" Adeline's eyes went wide. "No way."

"It's true."

"Does Caleb know this?"

Jesse nodded. "Yeah."

"He failed to mention that." Adeline crossed her arms. "No wonder the hunters kept finding us."

"He didn't want to scare you off. He couldn't escape without you."

Though she was still annoyed he hadn't told her, she understood why. She probably would've left him if she'd known. "Does the tracker work outside of this territory?"

"Yep. They've been tracking his every move since he left."

"I'm surprised they didn't catch him in the desert."

"The military can't leave without Ralock's permission." He threw a stick into the fire. "It takes a few days."

"So, the hunters couldn't chase after Caleb once he got out of here."

"Correct," he said, feeding another twig to the flames. "That's why he needed to get to the cabin before they reached him."

"Why the cabin?"

"It's the only place in this realm where he'd be safe."

Sadness overwhelmed her as she stared into the flames. She couldn't imagine the trauma Caleb had endured. "What was he like before he was trapped here?"

"He's growing on you, isn't he?" Jesse asked, his eyes twinkling with mischief.

Her cheeks went hot. "I'm just curious."

"I bet you are."

Adeline gave him a look. "Just tell me."

"Things were tough for Caleb when I first met him." Jesse looked back at the dying fire, his humor fading. "After a while, he turned into the kind of guy you could count on—loyal, dependable, and always fun."

"I can't imagine that."

"He's still that guy, Addie. It's just buried under a lot of pain, anger, and disappointment."

Adeline tried to picture it but couldn't. His rage was all she knew. "How did Ralock capture him?"

"He'll have to be the one to tell you."

"Why can't you?"

"Because it isn't my story to tell." Jesse stood, brushing the dirt from his pants. "Come on. Let's get moving."

Adeline winced as she climbed to her feet and picked the dead leaves from her jean shorts. She redid her messy bun, ignoring the lingering headache as she limped to the hiding spot.

Holding back a groan, she dipped her head inside the hideout and grabbed her bow and quiver. Another spasm of pain hit her body as she looped her quiver over her head and shouldered her bow.

It was going to be a rough day.

Jesse doused the remaining fire with water, sending a plume of smoke spiraling into the sky like a distress signal. If Ralock didn't know her location before, he did now.

Unfazed, Jesse slung his backpack over one shoulder, careful not to disturb his quiver. He turned to Adeline with a steady smile as smoke curled behind him. "Let's go save Caleb."

Chapter Twenty-Three

Sweat poured down Adeline's face as she hiked behind Jesse. The uphill climb was excruciating on her tired limbs, and the gnats swarming her face only worsened her sour mood. She'd never been so exhausted in her life.

"Where are we going?" she asked, shoving a branch out of her way.

"Caleb's in the city across the mountain," Jesse called over his shoulder.

A sudden surge of anxiety hit her. She knew little about that place, but she'd seen enough to know that it was crawling with Ralock's military and followers. How would she and Jesse navigate through it without getting caught?

"How are we going to get there?" she asked. "Ralock's warriors guard the tunnel that leads to the city."

"There's another way that no one knows about." Jesse climbed over a rock.

"Of course there is," she mumbled.

Weeds scratched her legs as they hiked through the wooded area, and her sweaty skin became a magnet for dirt. So did her soaked tank top. Swatting a bug from her face, Adeline grumbled as she walked through a patch of thick ferns. She couldn't wait to get out of the heat.

A distant noise made her perk up. It sounded like rushing water, growing louder as they pushed on.

Her thoughts immediately went to the poisonous lake she had nearly touched. She cringed. Hopefully, they wouldn't have to cross any water.

A roar of water filled the air. Adeline mounted a mossy boulder and squeezed through a giant mountain laurel. She stopped short, a gasp catching in her throat. A magnificent waterfall cascaded from the side of the mountain, crashing against the rocks below before rushing through the forest past her and Jesse. The sight was breathtaking, but she was still suspicious. Nothing in that territory could be trusted.

Jesse stepped to the water's edge, and Adeline panicked. "Don't touch it!"

"It's not poisonous," Jesse said, fighting a grin as he retrieved the water tin from his backpack.

"Are you sure?" Adeline asked, taking a cautious step forward.

"Positive." He dunked the tin into the water, filling it to the brim.

Adeline's shoulders slumped in relief as the cool mist from the waterfall tickled her overheated skin. She plunged her hands into the icy water and splashed her face. The cold felt incredible, leaving a tingling sensation as it dripped from her chin.

Jesse sealed the water tin and packed it away. "This is one of the few water sources that's still pure in this territory."

"Why is that?" she asked, rinsing the dirt from her arms.

"It was here before Ralock took over."

"I thought he had always been here."

"Nope. Ralock stole it years ago." Jesse plunged his entire head into the water, then whipped it up, flinging droplets like bullets.

"How?

"He tricked the rightful owner into handing over the territory," he said, brushing the water from his thick beard. "Ralock promised him wealth and power, then betrayed and murdered him."

"That's awful!"

Jesse flicked her a questioning glance. "Does that surprise you?"

"No, but it's still horrible."

"Ralock will be punished for his wickedness one day." Jesse rinsed the dry blood and dirt from his hands.

"When will that happen?"

"When it's supposed to."

Adeline left it at that; she was tired of talking about that monster.

They spent the next few minutes resting by the water. The rumbling waterfall soothed Adeline as she took a few slow sips of water. It was a relief to take a break.

"We've got to go up there." Jesse pointed to the falling water.

Adeline tilted her head back. "You want to go to the top?"

"Yep. There's a path."

Jesse began climbing the uneven stone steps that formed a winding path to the top. Shrubs and plants hindered sections of the slick rocks, but it looked manageable...as long as they didn't slip.

"Come on, Addie," he called over the rushing water.

Exhaling loudly, Adeline moved her tired body to climb the rocks. It didn't take long for her calves to burn and her breathing to turn ragged. Since there was no railing, she took her time, carefully ascending each step as the mist sprinkled against her.

By the time they reached the top of the natural staircase, they were practically standing next to the waterfall. It was deafening as it sprayed Adeline, sending chills down her body. She glanced down and nearly fainted. The massive boulders at the base of the waterfall looked like scattered pebbles. They wouldn't survive if they fell.

Jesse hugged the mountain wall and sidestepped toward the raging water until he disappeared behind it. Adeline bit her bottom lip and did the same, scooting after him.

Water pelted her as she pressed her hands against the rocks, their rough edges scraping against her palms. Inch by inch she went until she made it behind the falls, just in time to see Jesse slip into a gap in the mountainside. She went after him, sliding through the opening and into a tunnel.

The passageway was tight, with sharp rocks jutting from the walls like spikes. Drenched to the bone, Adeline saw sunlight gleaming beyond Jesse. It wouldn't take long to reach it.

"Where are we?" she asked, pivoting and twisting as she moved.

"A shortcut." Jesse ducked while splashing through a puddle.

The tunnel was short, but the last stretch was the hardest. Adeline squeezed through the narrow gap. A pointed rock dug into her stomach and snagged her tank top, tearing a hole as she wedged through. She didn't care; it was already ruined.

Jesse waited at the tunnel's exit, concealed by lush vegetation. Water dripped from his dirty T-shirt as he moved a large branch from their view. Warm sunlight peeked through as Adeline stood next to him, shivering.

They were still in the woods, on a mountain slope much like the one they'd left. The only difference was the bustling city below.

"Caleb's in that large cement building," Jesse said, pointing to the outskirts.

Adeline spotted it instantly. A real eyesore among all the brick buildings. "How are we supposed to get there?" she asked, squinting against the bright sun.

"I have a plan."

Jesse shoved aside a large branch and exited the tunnel. He held it in place until Adeline joined him.

The buzzing city permeated the air, triggering a sense of unease in Adeline. She shouldn't be afraid; she was with Jesse. And the full trees shielded them. Yet, her worry lingered.

"Follow me." Jesse hiked upward.

"Shouldn't we be going down there?"

"Nope," he said, his boots snapping a dead stick. "We have to go this way."

Adeline groaned. She really didn't want to hike up that mountain, but what choice did she have?

She forced her weary feet to follow, her wet socks squishing inside her sneakers. They weren't on a path, but Jesse seemed to know where he was going. His quiver, slung over his shoulder, knocked against his backpack as he hiked steadily through the forest.

They didn't have to go far before the trees ended, revealing an abandoned settlement overtaken by nature. Adeline recognized it immediately.

The old mine.

She was seeing it from a different angle, but she was positive it was the same place she'd been with Caleb. "Why are we here?"

"It's our way into the city. I'll show you." Jesse stepped out of the trees. "Wait here."

He pressed himself against an old house overrun with weeds and peeked around the corner. His eyes swept the area, darting left and right, before he vanished from Adeline's sight.

Holding her breath, Adeline kept looking behind her, nervously fidgeting with her quiver strap. Seconds dragged like minutes. She was tempted to go after him.

At last, Jesse came back into view. "Coast is clear," he said, waving her over.

Relief washed over Adeline as she moved to join him, carefully stepping around the chunks of metal along the ground. A lump formed in her throat when she spotted the rusted water pump.

What if we don't make it to him in time?

Thinking about it hurt more than she wanted to admit. When had she started caring so much about Caleb?

Jesse charged toward a small building nestled in the trees. Adeline assumed it was made of brick but couldn't tell with all the weeds. The undergrowth was thick, but Jesse plowed through it, moving around old barrels near the front door.

It was wide open, and they went right inside.

Sunlight streamed through the busted windows, revealing a messy living area coated in dust and grime. Every pane of glass was shattered, and the furniture lay overturned, as if a tornado had ripped through the space.

Jesse crunched through the broken glass and entered the adjoining room. Adeline quickly followed. The heavy, musty air made Adeline want to sneeze as she waited in the doorway, looking around the room. It was empty except for a tall bookshelf in the corner. Years of unread, dusty books lined its shelves. Most were average-sized novels crammed between books as thick as dictionaries.

Jesse headed directly to the crowded bookshelf. He inspected the books, tapping his chin thoughtfully before tracing his fingers along the worn spines. When he reached a certain book, he pressed on it until it sank into the shelf.

Click.

The entire bookshelf swung open on its side, just like the one Caleb had discovered.

Hurrying to Jesse's side, Adeline helped him pull the secret door fully open. Inside was a flight of long, spooky steps, nearly identical to the ones she and Caleb had used.

"Does this go to the underground tunnel Caleb and I found?" she asked.

"Yep."

"Why would we go back in there?"

"You'll see." Jesse patted her on the shoulder as he moved past her. "We'll need to use your dagger so we can see."

He entered the darkness as Adeline grabbed her dagger and tapped it on her palm. The glass blade lit up, casting light on the infinite staircase.

"Here we go again," she mumbled.

Chapter Twenty-Four

Stepping inside, Adeline let Jesse close the secret door behind her. The lock clicked shut, the sound bouncing eerily off the stone walls. A shiver rattled through her as the cold seeped into her bones. She raised her glowing dagger, its light cutting through the darkness. She wasn't looking forward to descending the long stairway.

Jesse took the lead without delay. The only sound was the steady tap of their footsteps echoing down the steps as they moved quickly.

Adeline was in agony again, her body screaming for a break, but she pushed through the pain until they reached the bottom.

There wasn't as much trash as before, though a few piles of junk were still thrown against the sides. Jesse didn't even glance at the clutter as he charged forward.

"Do you need the map?" Adeline asked, matching his strides.

"Nope." Jesse took a sharp right into another passageway.

How did he know the maze of tunnels so well? His steps were confident and precise as he turned into another passage. He'd been there before.

In no time, they arrived at another set of stairs. This one headed down.

"We're almost there," Jesse said, plunging down the stairway wrapped in blackness. He clearly wasn't afraid of the dark.

Adeline raced after him, the cold biting at her skin. She caught up, and they traveled together into the deep unknown. Down and down they went, their shadows bouncing on the walls. The steps seemed to have no end.

Where are we going?

Several minutes passed before the bottom of the stairs appeared. Adeline slowed, staring at the solid rock wall.

It was a dead end.

"You've got to be kidding me," Adeline huffed.

"You think I'd lead you to a dead end?"

She thrust a hand toward the wall. "You clearly did."

Jesse chuckled softly, shaking his head, as he approached the cave wall and ran his hand along the uneven surface. When he found a specific rock, he pressed the bottom with his index finger. Pebbles and dust fell from the ceiling as the wall in front of him rumbled. Adeline nearly bolted until the stone cracked open from the side.

Another secret door.

A tiny stream of light broke into the darkness. Adeline stood there, her mouth ajar. "How did you do that?"

"I pushed the hidden button." He turned to her, a grin touching his lips.

"There's a button?" She scanned the wall, seeing nothing but rocks. "I would've *never* figured that out."

"Good thing you've got me."

"Good thing." Adeline stepped onto ground level, her eyes on the sliver of light. "Where does it go?"

"The middle of the city."

"Why would you take us there?" she asked, her heart thudding faster. "Wouldn't it have been easier to sneak through the woods and go to the barracks?"

"It would've taken too long," Jesse said, adjusting his backpack strap. "We're short on time."

Adeline swallowed, her throat suddenly dry. "How much time do we have left?"

"Not much."

"We'd better go then."

Adeline went for the secret door, but Jesse caught her arm. "We can't go like this," he said, releasing her.

"Like what?" Adeline looked herself over. She was filthy, but why would that matter?

"It's broad daylight out there. We wouldn't get far."

Adeline made a face. "What are you talking about?"

"Hand me your dagger."

Confusion swept over her as Jesse extended his hand, his palm rough with calluses. Nothing he said made any sense, but there was no time to ask questions. She handed him the weapon, the glowing blade casting light over his plain features.

"Let me show you what else this dagger can do," he said.

Mischief coated his emerald eyes as he pressed the flat side of the glimmering blade into his palm. He counted to three. Then a white light exploded like a camera flash, blinding Adeline.

She rubbed her eyes until they adjusted to the sudden darkness. The only light now came from the secret door. It was enough to show that she was alone. Jesse was gone.

"Jesse?" she whispered in a trembling voice.

"I'm right here."

Adeline yelped as a warm hand gripped her shoulder. Jesse appeared in front of her like a ghost, holding her dagger that lit up the space again.

"What just happened?" she asked, placing a hand over her fluttering chest.

"I was invisible." He smiled, showing slightly uneven teeth.

"What? How?"

Jesse shrugged and handed the dagger back. "It just does."

Adeline lifted the weapon, watching the sparkles swirl inside the glass blade. She'd seen it do the impossible, but never once did she think it could make a person invisible. "Show me!"

"It's simple," he said. "Rest the blade in your palm for three seconds, and it'll turn you invisible."

Without hesitation, Adeline pressed the blade into her palm.

One. Two. Three.

A bright light flared from her shaky hand, flooding it with warmth. The flash vanished almost as quickly as it came, though her dagger continued to glow.

She didn't feel any different. Maybe it didn't work.

One glance at Jesse told her otherwise.

Black smoke swirled around him, rising in lazy spirals from his shoulders and head like he was smoldering.

"You're smoking!" Adeline exclaimed, her breath catching. "Why are you smoking?"

"I'm not invisible." Jesse looked through her. "Smoke rises from anyone who isn't invisible."

"This is so weird." Adeline watched the smoke curl around him. "Can you see me at all?"

"Nope," he said. "All I see is darkness."

"So cool!" Excitement bubbled within her. "I can't believe you never showed me this."

"You didn't need it until now."

"That's what you think."

Jesse let out a chuckle and touched her arm. Instantly, the smoke disappeared from him.

"What happened?" Adeline looked him over, searching for any trace of smoke.

"You'll lose your invisibility if someone touches you," he said. "Make sure you don't bump into anyone when we're out there."

"Got it."

"Another way you can lose it is if you drop your dagger."

"So I have to hold it the whole time I'm invisible?"

"Not necessarily," he said. "It just has to be touching you at all times; you can stash it in your sheath if you want."

"Are those the only ways to turn it off?"

"No. You can disable it yourself. Just press the blade into your palm again. After three seconds, you'll become visible."

"Okay," she said, drawing in a breath. "I think I've got it."

"I have to show you one more thing." Jesse retrieved his sword from his hip. "My sword can do the same thing."

He placed the blade into his palm, and a bright light burst from his weapon. Blinking rapidly, Adeline clutched her glowing dagger, seeing nothing but an empty staircase.

Jesse wasn't there.

"Turn on your invisibility," Jesse said, his voice bouncing along the walls.

A thrill shot through her as she pressed the flat of her dagger into her palm. Three seconds later, it lit up again. Jesse appeared before her, smirking, his outline barely visible beneath a soft white glow.

"Are you glowing?" Adeline asked, staring at the faint light shimmering off his weapons and backpack.

"Yep. Since I'm using the invisibility power too, I'll have a white light around me," he said. "Just like you."

Adeline glanced down at herself and gasped; she was glowing as well. She'd been too distracted to notice it before.

"Let me get this straight." She moved her hand around, watching the light radiate from her fair skin. "If someone is invisible like me, they glow. If they're not invisible, smoke rises from them?"

"Exactly," Jesse confirmed. "And since we're both invisible, we can touch each other without losing it."

To demonstrate, Jesse tapped her on the arm. Nothing happened. He was still glowing, and so was she.

"So strange."

"Any questions?"

Adeline was captivated by the light emanating from Jesse; he looked like a heavenly being. Her thoughts raced. She had questions. A lot of them. But they could wait.

"I don't think so," she said, shaking her head.

"Awesome. Let's go."

Sheathing his sword, Jesse approached the cracked door, a warm glow traveling behind him. Adeline carefully turned off her dagger's light and slid it into its golden sheath as reality settled over her. Soon, they'd be navigating a perilous city swarming with Ralock's army and followers.

Fear and worry warred within her. Getting caught would mean death.

Shaking the thought away, Adeline took a calming breath as Jesse opened the secret door.

Chapter Twenty-Five

The potent smell of tobacco burned Adeline's lungs as she left the tunnel and entered a living area bathed in the afternoon sun. A cough threatened, but she held it back as Jesse slid the secret bookshelf door back into place.

She cringed at the shaggy orange carpet and lime green wallpaper, both coated with nicotine stains. An old turn-dial television sat in front of a battered couch with more holes than she could count. It felt like she'd stepped into the 1970s.

Approaching footsteps sent her heart to flight. She pressed her back against the wall next to Jesse right as a skinny, middle-aged man entered from the foyer, smoke rising from his body. He was skin and bones, with a receding hairline and deep wrinkles that aged him by twenty years.

The man reeked of urine and booze as he staggered toward the old television with a half-empty bottle in hand. A cigarette dangled from his lips as he turned the dial until a strange sitcom flickered on the screen. He stumbled to the sofa and plopped down. Liquor splashed across his lap, followed by an explicit word. The man's neck flushed red as he patted the wet spot on his dirty shorts and took a long drag from the cigarette.

It was a pitiful sight.

"We interrupt this program for an important message from our master," a masculine voice announced from the television.

Ralock's face took over the screen, his short black hair styled to perfection. He looked handsome, even with the deep scar running the length of his cheek, but the sight of him made Adeline's blood run cold.

"Greetings, my faithful followers," Ralock said smoothly. "It has come to my attention that we have a dangerous fugitive in our midst."

A sketch of a teenage girl filled the screen, and Adeline lost the ability to breathe.

It was her.

The pencil drawing was disturbingly accurate. From her deep blue eyes to the faint freckles across the bridge of her nose. Everything about it looked just like her. Even the waves in her auburn hair were spot-on.

"This girl goes by the name Adeline Bigsby," Ralock said, the sketch still displayed. "She's extremely dangerous and must be brought into custody. I'm offering a reward to anyone who brings her to me—dead or alive. The one who brings me this vile criminal will receive three hot meals a day at Drop Dead Diner for the next month. If anyone has any information about her whereabouts, report to my warriors immediately."

The screen went black, then switched back to the previous program.

Adeline shot Jesse a fearful look. *"Why is Ralock looking for me?"*

"He wants to kill you," he replied, his words sinking deep into her thoughts.

Her stomach knotted. *"Why?"*

"You cut his face, remember?" Jesse's mouth curved with amusement as he glanced at the weapon resting on her hip. *"Plus, you're deadly with that dagger."*

The compliment was nice, but it didn't help much. Her mind was consumed with the broadcast. Now everyone in the territory would be looking for her.

Jesse raised a finger to his lips before pointing to the foyer. *"Let's move."*

He tiptoed across the room, past the intoxicated man, who was slumping deeper into the sofa. His eyes fluttered as he dozed off, clueless that he had company.

Jesse reached the foyer and motioned for Adeline. Her pulse thundered. It was her turn.

Holding her breath, she crept forward, her sneakers sinking into the shaggy carpet. Once she reached Jesse, he pointed to the narrow staircase leading to the second floor. He went first, the stairs creaking beneath his weight.

Anxiety clawed at Adeline's throat as she glanced back at the owner of the house. He hadn't moved, his soft snores showing he was asleep. She relaxed a little as she climbed the steps, careful not to make too much noise. When she reached the second level, she found Jesse in a nearby bedroom. It smelled just as bad as the rest of the house, with faded wallpaper peeling from the walls. A thick layer of dust covered the outdated furniture. No one had been in there for a long time.

Jesse went to the window and rolled up the dusty blinds. Dust particles danced in the air as warm sunlight entered the small room. Using his hand, he wiped a portion of the grimy window before pressing his face against the glass.

The floor groaned as Adeline snuck to the window to peek outside.

Stunned, she could only stare, her heartbeat loud and frantic.

Rows of brick houses and shops lined both sides of the cobblestone road, which was packed with people. A shabby bakery, thrift store, and butchery were among the stores she could see, along with a rowdy bar with outdoor seating. It was a bustling downtown, but its neglect and extreme security measures made it look more like a prison.

Iron bars guarded every window and door, and armed warriors patrolled the area on horseback. Their black armor glistened in the sun as they trotted down the road, ignoring the dire need of the people around them.

Adeline's heart sank. She had never seen so many homeless people in one place. Beggars lined the sidewalks while others dug through overflowing trash cans. But they weren't the only ones who were deathly thin and dressed in tattered clothes.

Almost everyone she saw looked malnourished, like they were one meal away from death. Only the warriors appeared healthy. They varied in shape and size, but it was clear they had been well cared for.

"How are we supposed to walk through there without someone bumping into us?" Adeline whispered, her eyes on the busy street.

"Easy. Don't run into anyone."

Adeline punched his arm. "I'm being serious, Jesse."

"So am I."

She rolled her eyes as she observed the activity outside. They'd have to be extremely careful out there.

Jesse pointed to a tall structure rising above the row of brick buildings. "That's where Caleb is."

Weathered cement blocks formed the narrow tower that reached the sky. It had windows on every level, each guarded with thick metal bars.

"How exactly are we supposed to get him out of there?" she asked, frowning.

"Just wait and see," Jesse said, heading back toward the stairs.

Adeline stared at the hectic street, stress rising in her. It was intimidating from a distance; she couldn't imagine it up close.

She took a much-needed breath before leaving the bedroom. Jesse was waiting for her at the stairs. His quick grin didn't calm her fears, and neither did the loud creaking of the steps as they descended.

The television still blared from the living room as they snuck down the tight hallway leading to a messy kitchen. It reeked of mold and garbage, and Adeline quickly saw why.

Dark circles stained the ceiling, and Adeline couldn't see the bottom of the sink or the counter thanks to a mountain of dirty dishes. Cigarette butts and trash were all over the place, along with an infestation of cockroaches.

Adeline followed Jesse to the sliding glass door, her stomach churning as she accidentally squished an unlucky roach. The glass was filthy, but she could still make out the fenced backyard. It was small and overgrown, with knee-high grass bending with the breeze.

"We've got to be quick," Jesse said, lifting the latch. "Follow my lead."

He slid open the door, and a gust of wind rushed inside. Adeline gagged at the vile stench. It smelled like feces and death. There was no escaping it.

"I'm going to be sick." She stormed past Jesse.

As soon as her sneakers touched the grass, she doubled over and vomited. Her stomach heaved until nothing remained but dry spasms, leaving her throat raw and burning.

"Are you all right?" Jesse asked, touching her shoulder.

"I think so." Adeline wiped her mouth. "What is that awful smell?"

"You don't want to know."

Adeline cringed as the city raged beyond the shabby wooden fence. It leaned at an angle, collapsing on one side with several boards missing. The tall weeds made it hard to see through the gaps.

"Stay close," Jesse said in a whisper.

He parted the weeds with his lean body, heading straight for the gate hanging crookedly from its hinges. Adeline's stomach was in knots as she trailed after him.

The old gate whined as Jesse pulled it open, but the sound was lost in the rush of people hurrying down the road, heads down. No one noticed.

Glancing both ways, Jesse stepped onto the spacious sidewalk and beckoned for Adeline to follow.

The thumping in her chest amplified as she moved onto the uneven cobblestones and took in the chaos around her. The air was thick and oppressive, like a suffocating fog. So much was happening at once that she stood paralyzed.

Their sidewalk was quieter than the one across the street, which was lined with businesses. But it couldn't compare to the hordes of people flooding the road between them. There were no vehicles in sight, only undernourished people going about their day. Smoke curled off their bodies, and each one bore the same cobra tattoo Caleb had on his forearm.

Stray dogs barked as they weaved between the people, who seemed incapable of smiling. Every face wore either anger or despair. Nothing in between.

Jesse yanked Adeline back right as a sweaty man hustled by. His stench hung heavy as Adeline braced herself against the fence, her heart racing. *"Thanks."*

Jesse nodded and motioned for her to stay put while he studied the flow of traffic. They were far back enough to avoid most people, but they still had to be careful.

As Adeline waited for his signal, something moved in her peripheral vision. Turning her head, she saw a piece of paper flapping from a power pole. Her stomach curled. It was a wanted sign with the same sketch of her she'd seen on television.

And it wasn't just there. It was everywhere. Windows, storefronts, and doors were covered with her face. There were even some flyers scattered along the road as if they'd been thrown into the wind.

Trying to stay calm, Adeline looked back at the power pole with her face on it. A nauseating mix of fear and disbelief flooded her as she locked eyes with the wanted flyer.

She startled when she noticed an old man slumped against the pole beneath the flyer. He'd been sitting so still she hadn't noticed him. He stared at his lap, his face hidden beneath a curtain of long, unwashed hair.

A sudden burst of wind lifted a section of his graying hair, and Adeline nearly screamed.

Half of his face was gone. One of his eyes was missing, and birds had pecked his cheek clean to the bone.

Nausea surged up. Adeline covered her mouth and turned away. It took her a second to regain her composure. "I can't do this, Jesse."

"You have to." Jesse continued to watch the road. "Caleb needs us."

"This place is horrible."

"What did you expect?"

"Not this." She pointed to the dead man.

Jesse's face fell when he saw the body. "I know this is hard, but we have to keep going."

He turned back to the crowded road while Adeline shuddered beside him. Her thoughts went to Caleb. How had he survived this place? Everywhere she looked was chaotic.

"We've got to cross the street, but it's too busy here," Jesse said softly.

"So, what do we do?"

"We need to find an opening." Jesse started to move. "Follow me."

He booked it down the sidewalk, his shoulder brushing the brick wall. Adeline darted after him. Endless garbage crunched under her sneakers as she shadowed his every move.

They stopped and hugged the wall anytime someone passed, then continued onward until the sidewalk ended at a rundown, boarded-up house.

One glance at the hectic road and her knees nearly buckled. It was just as crowded as before. Maybe worse. Plus, there was a busy bar directly across from them. A long line stretched outside, and people pushed and shoved to get in.

"You want to cross here?" Adeline asked.

"Yes. Just wait."

"For what?"

Two guys in line started fighting. They were both dangerously thin and clearly intoxicated, hollering at each other with slurred rage. The taller one shoved the other into the middle of the street and threw the first punch.

All surrounding activity stopped as a crowd swarmed the fight, including three warriors on horseback. But instead of breaking it up, the warriors egged them on, shouting encouragement and placing bets as the fight escalated.

"Let's go." Jesse took off across the street, keeping his distance from the growing mob.

Adeline sprinted after him, the hoots and hollers of the crowd ringing in her ears. Pumping her arms, she cringed as the sickening crack of breaking bones cut through the commotion. She didn't dare look back.

She leaped onto the empty walkway and followed Jesse, who hustled in the opposite direction of the brawl. He tossed her a quick glance over his shoulder as he jogged down the long cobbled path. The noise of the crowd still blared behind them as they ducked into an alley and slowed their pace.

Trembling, Adeline walked directly behind Jesse, hyper-aware of her surroundings. Their steps were quick and deliberate as they avoided the overflowing dumpsters and homeless people sleeping against the buildings. Smoke curled from their thin bodies as they slept along the cobblestones.

Adeline's blood pumped faster as the alley led them to another street. It resembled the one they'd just left but was far quieter. Residential houses lined both sides. There wasn't a business in sight.

"Come on," Jesse said.

He waited for a tiny, angry woman to pass before crossing the street. A soft glow beamed from him as he jogged, his sword knocking against his thigh.

Adeline tore after him as broken glass cracked underfoot. They raced down the sidewalk and quickly reached the final house bordering the woods.

Tree limbs whipped against them as they moved between the rundown house and the woods, following a strip of grass no wider than a game trail. The cement barracks came into view and seemed to grow as Adeline hurried. Fear for Caleb gnawed at her with every step.

"Hang on, Caleb," she said in a whisper. "We're almost there."

Chapter Twenty-Six

The lively city buzzed in the background as Adeline and Jesse neared the barracks. It was heavily guarded with iron bars thicker than her fist. Warriors patrolled the premises on foot, and hunters were stationed along the roof with crossbows. It looked impenetrable.

Adeline started to sweat. How would they get inside?

Jesse held out his hand, stopping her. *"Caleb's in the basement. Before we get him, I need those keys."*

"What keys?"

Jesse pointed to the hunter posted at the front door. He was lounging in a metal chair with his legs crossed, reading a magazine. Smoke rose from his body as he flipped the page, irritation etched into his camouflaged face.

Something dangled at his side. A ring of skeleton keys hung from the belt loop of his tactical pants.

"Wait here," Jesse said.

Adeline held her breath as Jesse crept forward, easily slipping past the warriors patrolling the entrance. He snuck up the steps undetected and inched toward the hunter. Crouching low, he reached for the keys.

Cling!

The keys rattled softly, jingling like a wind chime. Jesse froze in place.

The hunter shifted, tilting his head slightly and flaring his nostrils as if catching a scent.

A jolt of fear shot through Adeline as his gaze lifted, sweeping the area with slow precision.

For a moment, she thought he sensed Jesse's presence. But his snake-like eyes dropped back to the magazine in his hands.

Moving with deliberate care, Jesse unhooked the key ring from the man's waistband. A soft beam of light glowed around the keys, confirming their invisibility, as Jesse tucked them into his pocket. He gave Adeline a quick thumbs-up and a triumphant smile before tiptoeing down the steps.

Instead of heading back to her, Jesse veered toward the side of the building facing the thick forest. He waved for her to follow before slipping out of view.

Anxiety struck Adeline as she looked both ways before bolting after him. The arrows in her quiver clacked together, but not loudly enough to raise suspicion.

She rounded the barracks and rushed to Jesse. He was on his knees, yanking on a set of iron bars that guarded a filthy window. The glass was too grimy to see through, but she was confident it led to the basement. The metal frame whined with each tug as the bolts loosened.

Adeline stood guard, her breath catching with each creak of metal. No warriors were in sight, but that could change at any moment.

Screech!

The frame ripped out of the wall, making Adeline jump. Her hand flew to her dagger as she looked around wildly. Surely someone had heard that. She held her breath, her ears straining for the rush of boots. A shout. Anything. Glancing both ways, she kept her weapon sheathed, her palm growing damp against the hilt.

But no one came.

Jesse gently set the metal piece aside. Before Adeline could calm down, he kicked the window. It shattered, glass spilling into the basement.

She stared at him in bewilderment. So much for being quiet.

Again, she scanned the area as Jesse used his boot to knock the remaining shards from the window frame. Once it was clear, he handed Adeline his bow. *"Hold this."*

Dropping to his stomach, Jesse shimmied backward, his feet disappearing through the broken window. He barely fit as his backpack scraped the top of the frame.

Adeline stood alone, gripping the bow tighter.

"Hand me the bows," Jesse said, hidden from view.

A cold sweat slicked Adeline's palms as she knelt at the opening. She could barely make out Jesse as she pushed both bows through the busted window. The drop was farther than she'd expected.

Lying on her stomach, she scooted backward. Cold air licked her legs as they dangled inside the basement. She didn't overthink it and let herself drop.

Jesse caught her midair and set her gently on the cement floor.

Goosebumps trailed up Adeline's arms as she reached over her head to make sure the arrows were still in her quiver while scanning the eerie basement. The only source of light was coming from the busted window they'd entered through. It wasn't overly bright, but bright enough to give her a preview of the basement. It was big and bare, with cement blocks making up the walls. All she could see was a closed door to her left and a plain flight of steps leading to another closed door above. A sliver of light leaked from beneath both.

"Caleb's in there," Jesse said, pointing to the nearby door with Adeline's bow before handing it to her.

"Okay. Let's grab him and get out of here." She hooked her bow over her shoulder and moved to step forward.

Jesse caught her wrist, holding her back. "He's in bad shape, Addie. Real bad shape."

Tears stung her eyes, and she swallowed the sudden lump in her throat.

"I need you to be brave," he said gently, releasing her wrist. "He's been tortured and isn't in his right mind."

A bloodcurdling scream shattered the silence. Adeline scrambled against the wall, her heart beating erratically. It came from the closed door; it had to be Caleb.

A second scream rang out, followed by another voice that wasn't Caleb's.

Adeline couldn't move. What were they doing to him?

An instant later, the door burst open, smashing into the wall. The basement shook as a stout warrior with cornrows stormed out. The darkness of his skin and armor helped him blend into the shadows as he charged up the stairs and disappeared through the door, slamming it shut behind him.

"We've got to hurry," Jesse said, vanishing into the dimly lit room.

Adeline's breathing wouldn't slow as she forced herself to follow. A pitiful moan filled her ears. It amplified with each step. She choked back tears as she crept to the threshold, terrified of what she'd find inside.

Chapter Twenty-Seven

ALL THE AIR LEFT Adeline's lungs when she peeked inside the room. Freezing at the doorway, she grabbed the doorframe for support as the overpowering stench of blood struck her nostrils. Her stomach lurched as she took in the small space lit by a single swinging bulb.

Blood splattered the concrete walls, and a pool of it drained slowly through the grate in the center of the floor. A skinny male was slumped against the far wall, his head bowed. He was bloody and beaten, with his arms chained above his head.

It took Adeline a moment to realize it was Caleb. His hair had been buzzed off, and he was shirtless. Bruises covered his body, and his ribs were visible beneath his skin. Among the bruises were scars. Lots of scars. They ranged in size and covered his entire torso. Most were discolored, showing their age. He'd had them for a while.

Tears clouded Adeline's vision as her gaze swept over his battered body. He looked like death. *How are we going to get him out of here?*

Caleb was staring at his lap, mumbling to himself, as Jesse crouched next to him.

"Caleb," Jesse whispered. "We're here to rescue you."

Caleb slowly lifted his bloody head, revealing a deep gash that ran up the side of his neck. His head rocked as if he'd been drugged as he fought to open his black eyes. One was swollen shut, but the other blinked open.

He did a slow sweep of the room before bellowing out an ear-piercing scream.

Terror gripped Adeline as Caleb thrashed against his chains. The iron links rattled against the wall but stayed locked in place. His scream dissolved into violent coughing, each gasp sounding like he was choking on air.

Angry footsteps stomped above, shaking the swaying bulb. Someone was coming.

Boots thudded down the stairs, and Adeline launched herself against the wall. Jesse did the same as a warrior barged into the room.

It was the same man as before, only now he carried a metal rod.

"Shut up!" he barked, striking Caleb in the stomach.

Caleb doubled over, his head hanging limply as he wheezed for air.

"We have to do something, Jesse!" Adeline bit back a cry as tears poured down her cheeks.

Jesse shook his head, tears pooling in his green eyes. *"Not yet."*

The warrior placed the rod under Caleb's chin, forcing him to look up. "It's a pity your friend didn't come," he said, his voice low and dark. "I guess she didn't think you were worth it."

Lowering the rod, he spat on Caleb before leaving. The door slammed shut, and the warrior stormed upstairs.

Caleb was still rasping, with his head slumped forward. Death was knocking at his door. Adeline feared they were too late to save him.

That could've been me. She wiped her damp cheeks.

Jesse approached Caleb again, but this time he gently touched his arm. The white glow around him vanished, replaced by curling smoke.

Adeline went still. He was no longer invisible.

"Caleb," Jesse whispered.

Caleb slowly raised his head. His one good eye filled with rage before he let out another piercing scream. He kicked and squirmed like he was trying to strike Jesse, but the chains kept his arms in place.

"Calm down," Jesse said firmly, "or that warrior will come back."

Caleb yelled even louder as he wrestled against the iron shackles. They clanked together, digging into his injured wrists. Fresh blood trickled over his cobra tattoo.

Why is he acting this way? Adeline pushed down her own anger. *We're trying to help him!*

Her ears were still ringing even after his screaming stopped. There was no doubt the warrior had heard him. Everyone in the barracks probably had. Yet nobody came. They were either too busy or simply tired of dealing with him.

"I have to remove his tattoo before releasing him," Jesse whispered.

"How are you going to do that?" Adeline asked.

"You'll see," he said. "But first, cover his mouth."

"I can't touch him," Adeline said, panic lacing her words. "He'll scream the second he sees me."

"He's going to scream no matter what," he said calmly. "That's why you're going to cover his mouth."

Adeline broke into a cold sweat as she glanced back at Caleb. He was out of it, swinging his head back and forth while mumbling nonsense to himself. "All right."

Taking a deep breath, she stepped around the puddle of blood and stationed herself on the opposite side of Caleb. She gave Jesse a nod when she was ready.

In a swift move, she pressed her hands against his busted lips. The smoke around Caleb vanished as he snapped his head toward her. His good eye went wide, and he latched onto her hand, his teeth sinking deep into her skin.

"Ouch!" Adeline pulled away, her hand throbbing. She tried to cover his mouth again, but he whipped around like a wild beast, yelling at the top of his lungs.

"Cover his mouth," Jesse said, his jaw set tightly.

Smashing his head against the wall, Caleb kept screaming as he yanked at the chains embedded in the cement. Adeline slammed her hand over his mouth, silencing him. He thrashed beneath her grip, yelling into her palm, but she didn't let go. She wasn't going to let him bite her again.

As she fought to keep him quiet, Jesse clamped his hand over Caleb's forearm, directly over the dark tattoo.

A burst of white light flashed from Jesse's palm, and Caleb instantly relaxed. He stopped screaming and flailing and went completely still, like he'd been shot with a tranquilizer.

Jesse removed his hand, and Adeline gasped.

The tattoo was gone.

She peeled her hand from Caleb's mouth; she couldn't believe it. There was no evidence the tattoo had ever been there.

Reaching into his pocket, Jesse pulled out the ring of keys he'd stolen. They jingled as he shuffled through them. Once he found the right one, he inserted it into the keyhole.

With one soft click, the shackles released Caleb's wrists. His arms dropped to his sides as he slumped over, his chin pinned to his chest. He looked dead, but he was still breathing as Jesse pressed his water tin to Caleb's lips.

"Drink," Jesse said, helping Caleb tilt his head back.

Most of the water rolled down his chin, but he managed to drink some. When the tin was empty, Jesse set it aside and gently leaned Caleb's head back against the wall.

It took Caleb a moment to open his bruised eye. He squinted at Jesse, his body shuddering with each strained breath. Confusion swept across his face. "Jesse? Where am I?"

"Ralock captured you yesterday."

Groaning, Caleb closed his eye. It took him a while to speak. "Did Ralock find Adeline?"

"No, she's right here."

Caleb struggled to open his eye again, but quickly sealed it when he saw Adeline. "You were supposed to stay in that tree."

"And you were supposed to go to the cabin with me," she said, blinking back tears.

His split lip curved slightly. "Touché."

Adeline caught a glimpse of his teeth, and her stomach dropped. A front one was missing. Someone must have knocked it out.

"I need to check your ribs," Jesse said, kneeling beside him. He carefully probed each rib while Caleb gritted his teeth. His face twisted in anguish with each touch.

"You've got two fractured ribs." Jesse dropped his hand. "That's why it hurts to breathe."

Caleb groaned. "Fantastic."

Hopelessness plowed into Adeline. She desperately wanted to help, but what could she do? Her dagger was useless against anything but open wounds.

"I can heal them," Jesse said.

"I don't want your help," Caleb wheezed.

"You won't make it out of here alive if I don't help."

Caleb sagged against the wall, gasping for breath. "I don't care anymore."

"Well, I do."

"Leave me alone, Jesse. You've done enough damage."

Adeline's mouth dropped open. Fury ripped through her. Caleb was giving up? After everything they'd done for him?

"Listen here, Caleb." She grabbed his chin, making him look at her. "I don't know what your problem is with Jesse, nor do I care, but we risked our lives to rescue you."

"You shouldn't have come here." Caleb pulled away. "Leave while you still can."

"I'm *not* leaving without you."

Caleb stared at her, his brows scrunching. "Why do you want to help me?"

"Because that's what friends do."

Caleb blinked, unable to hide the shock on his face or the moisture forming in his good eye. He went silent, processing her words. After what seemed like forever, he whispered, "I don't trust him."

"Do you trust me?" she asked.

Caleb didn't look away for a long moment, his face an unreadable mix of emotion. Finally, he nodded.

"Then let him help you."

Dropping eye contact, Caleb fought to breathe while staring at his battered chest. Seconds stretched on in silence before he whispered, "Okay."

Jesse stepped in. "This will only take a second," he said as he placed both palms on Caleb's ribcage.

Caleb jolted as if he'd been electrocuted, his eye widening with disbelief. He touched his ribs, his breathing smooth and steady. "How'd you do that?"

"No time to explain." Jesse stood. "It's time to move."

Adeline helped Caleb to his feet as Jesse pulled a clean shirt from his backpack. Caleb raised his arms with a moan, and they carefully slipped the loose cotton tee over his head.

As the fabric fell, Adeline caught sight of his back and stilled. Deep, aged scars ran the length of it, worse than the ones on his chest. They were large and jagged, as if someone had carved his flesh with a knife. She resisted the urge to cry.

What happened to you?

She wanted to know his story, to know about his life in the Dark Territory. More tears surfaced, but she shook them away. She didn't want Caleb to know she'd seen his back.

"Are you able to walk?" Adeline asked.

"I think so," Caleb said. "They must've hit my face more than my legs."

Adeline observed his black eyes and swollen cheeks, and her frown deepened. She couldn't begin to fathom his pain.

"Where are we?" Caleb asked, scanning the grim room.

"We're in the barracks," Jesse said.

Caleb's face turned deathly pale. "The tall cement one?"

"Yep, that's the one."

Caleb looked between them. "How are we getting out of here?"

"The same way we got in." Jesse drew his sword.

Discomfort crossed Caleb's battered face as he focused on the silver-edged blade. "You want to fight Ralock's military?"

"Nope. I have a better idea." Jesse grinned as he placed the blade in his palm. In a flash, he disappeared.

Caleb jumped, whipping his head around the room. "Where did he go?"

Jesse reappeared with a smirk. "I was invisible."

Caleb staggered back, nearly tripping over himself. "How did you do that?"

"Both of our weapons can make us invisible," Jesse explained. "They can make you invisible too, as long as you're holding on to one of us."

Making a face, Caleb kept his eye on Jesse's long blade. "You can make me invisible?"

"Yes," Jesse said, his gaze steady.

"How?"

"There's no time to explain." Jesse held out his hand. "We have to go now."

Disgust contorted Caleb's features. "I'm not holding your hand. That's weird."

"You can hold on to my backpack instead," Jesse said, turning his back to him. "But do *not* let go. You'll turn visible if you do."

Caleb hesitated, then reached for the backpack strap.

Glancing back, Jesse made sure Caleb had a firm grip before turning to Adeline. "You ready?"

Adeline extracted her dagger and rested it against her palm. "Yep."

Chapter Twenty-Eight

Light flashed inside the grungy room, leaving Adeline and her friends with a gentle glow. They were invisible and ready to go.

Blood coated the soles of Jesse's boots as he went to the door, tugging Caleb behind him. Caleb nearly tripped over his own shoes, his attention fixed on Adeline.

"Why are you glowing?" he asked, giving her a bewildered look.

"Because I'm invisible." She stashed her weapon. "Everyone else out there will have smoke rising off their bodies."

Caleb looked at the light surrounding Jesse and the backpack before holding up his own glowing hand. "All of us glow because we're invisible?"

"Yes," Adeline confirmed.

"One more quick rule," Jesse said, tucking his sword away. "Do not let *anyone* touch you. That'll make you visible again."

"Okay." Caleb kept his eye on his free hand, moving it around as the faint glow flickered around his fingers.

The door opened with a creak, and Jesse peeked into the quiet basement before stepping through. Adeline trailed behind Caleb, her nerves rattling as they made their way to the broken window. Sunlight touched her face as she craned her neck upward. It was way too high; they'd need a ladder to reach it.

"How are we supposed to get up there?" Caleb asked, anxiety thick in his voice.

The basement door swung open, and hefty footsteps pounded down the steps.

Startled by the approaching sound, Adeline hurried to the back of the basement with Jesse and Caleb. They waited, their chests rising and falling in sync, as the warrior with cornrows appeared.

He strutted toward the vacant room, unhurried, tapping a rod against his palm like he was itching to use it. As he stepped through the doorway, a terrifying roar tore through the silence.

"The prisoner escaped," he bellowed, spinning on his heel. "The prisoner escaped!"

He sprinted through the basement and thundered up the stairs.

The once-quiet barracks was now in turmoil. The ceiling shook as angry voices shouted over one another.

"Don't move," Jesse whispered.

Rigid and tense, Adeline waited, her hands clenched and heart pounding. A suffocating heaviness settled over the room, as if the air itself had been laced with fear. Caleb must've felt it too. He trembled uncontrollably. The only one who seemed immune to it was Jesse. He looked calm as he watched the steps, a serious expression fixed on his bearded face.

A stampede of boots boomed down the steps. The basement shook with the sound. Ralock entered first, followed by four warriors—two women and two men, each with a look that could kill.

Ralock's polished Oxfords tapped against the floor as he marched into the adjacent room, his warriors following behind. "How did he escape?" he demanded.

"Someone unlocked his cuffs," a deep voice answered as the chains rattled.

"Bigsby," Ralock growled. "Find them!"

All the air rushed from Adeline's lungs as Ralock and his warriors scanned the open basement. She stood frozen as they looked every which way.

"Look, the window!" A blond-haired warrior pointed. "They must have escaped through it."

"I want all personnel searching for them," Ralock said, balling his fists. "No one sleeps until they're found!"

"Yes, Master," the warriors said in unison.

The warriors scurried upstairs while Ralock took his time. He ascended the steps with an arrogant strut, his expensive shoes clicking against the stairs.

Being near him made it difficult to breathe. Adeline was glad when he was no longer in sight. "What do we do now?" she asked as the shouting above intensified.

"We're going upstairs," Jesse said in a whisper.

"Upstairs?" Her voice cracked. "That's where everyone is!"

"It's the only way out."

"What about one of the other windows?" Caleb's words came in a shaky rush.

"Guards are in front of them now." Jesse started moving toward the stairway. "Upstairs is our only option."

A look of sheer terror flashed across Caleb's face. He glanced back at Adeline before Jesse propelled him forward. His steps were sluggish, but he didn't complain as he held on to the backpack. He was moving better than expected, considering the shape he was in.

Adeline stayed close, struggling to calm her rising nerves. They paused when they reached the stairway, light pouring from the top. The door had been left open.

Armed hunters and warriors hustled by, their combat boots pounding across the hardwood floor. A shiver ran down Adeline's back. There were so many of them. It would take a miracle to escape.

Jesse didn't look afraid, but cautious, as he gripped the railing and tested the first step. The old board creaked under his weight, but it wasn't overly loud. He crept upward, with Caleb limping after him. Adeline wasn't far behind, her sneakers squeaking softly with each step.

Halfway up the stairs, the light dimmed.

Someone was standing in the doorway.

"I'm going to check the basement again," the warrior said, her silhouette revealing a fit physique.

Adeline stood immobile, her knuckles turning white as she clutched the railing. They had nowhere to go.

Before the woman could take a step, another warrior grabbed her bicep. "Stop wasting time; we've already checked down there."

The warrior was dragged from view, barking insults at her colleague. Her quick steps and venomous voice faded as light returned to the stairway.

Adeline released the breath she'd been holding.

An unnerving silence fell as they waited. Ralock's military no longer rushed by. Most of them were probably outside. At least that was what Adeline hoped for as they snuck up the stairs.

No one was around when they reached the first floor, revealing a basic lounge. It looked as old as it smelled, with overused couches facing a brick fireplace coated in soot. Two hallways branched off on either side.

Jesse quickly chose the one on the right. Doors lined the long corridor, each marked with a two-digit number above the frame. It reminded Adeline of a hotel.

Shuffling down the hall, she wondered what was behind each door. Her heart rate quickened at the sound of distant voices. She couldn't pinpoint where they were coming from, but they were getting louder.

An open door came into view, and irritated voices came from within. Jesse and Caleb rushed past, but Adeline paused at the threshold.

The space was large, like a conference room, with tall windows overlooking the city. A massive table sat in the center. It could easily fit a dozen people.

The warrior who had struck Caleb stood hunched over a map spread across the center of the table. A hunter stood beside him.

"They can't be far," the camo-faced hunter said. "The prisoner hasn't been gone long."

"They're probably hiding somewhere in the city, waiting for nightfall," the warrior said, still examining the map.

"There are endless places to hide here." The hunter pounded his fist on the table. "And now that his tracker isn't working, it'll be impossible to find him."

The warrior smacked the hunter on the back of his head. "The master will have our heads if they escape the territory. Stop making excuses and track them down!"

Adeline hustled toward Jesse and Caleb, who were already at the end of the hall. Caleb's face whitened with fear as he frantically motioned for her to follow before being forced through a doorway.

Shooting a quick glance over her shoulder, Adeline watched the warrior and hunter leave the conference room, heading the other way. Once they were out of sight, she slipped into the final room and softly shut the door behind her.

She turned. And froze.

A single bed sat in the room, its white sheets tucked tightly into a metal frame. It resembled a hospital bed, with iron chains dangling on either side. The room contained nothing else except a barred window.

Who'd they keep in here? She stared at the chains. *And why?*

Adeline's thoughts spiraled as Jesse stood at the window, prying the latch open. He raised the window all the way up. A light breeze blew inside, giving them a taste of freedom.

Glancing out, Adeline was relieved to see how close they were to the ground. The forest was also nearby, offering a potential hiding place. The only thing standing in their way was the iron bars.

Jesse grabbed the thick metal rods and shook them. Nothing happened. They were bolted firmly into the cement and weren't going anywhere. Releasing the bars, he looked at Adeline. "Use your dagger to cut them. I'll watch the door."

"How?" Adeline asked, a tremor in her voice.

"Press the blade against the top and bottom of each one; it'll burn through them." He turned toward the door, forcing Caleb to shift.

Caleb still hadn't said a word. He shivered uncontrollably, glancing back at Adeline as loud voices boomed outside. No one had noticed the open window...yet.

Jesse removed the bow from his shoulder and loaded it with an arrow as Adeline went to work. She pressed the blade to the top of the first rod and applied pressure. The metal melted away like wax. It was almost too easy.

Gripping the middle of the rod, she pressed the dagger to the bottom. It burned through just as quickly, and she nearly dropped the heavy piece as she set it by her feet.

One down, six to go.

Adeline went to the next bar and effortlessly sliced through it, setting it on the floor. It landed with a soft thud as she moved to the next. Like clockwork, she removed each barrier until she reached the last one.

Loud footsteps echoed beyond the door, making her freeze.

"Don't stop, Addie," Jesse whispered, drawing back his bowstring.

Adrenaline coursed through Adeline as she went back to the last bar. The approaching steps pounded in her ears as she melted the upper part of the rod.

The door swung open, and in walked a warrior.

Adeline's heart jumped at the sight of the stout man with thick arms. Dark brown hair framed his harsh face, which hardened when he saw the open window.

"I found something!" he yelled, turning to fetch backup.

Jesse's arrow slammed into his head, dropping him to the floor. Blood oozed from the fatal wound.

"Hurry!" Jesse urged.

Shouts rumbled down the hall right as Adeline sliced through the bottom of the final rod. She dropped it on the floor. "It's open."

"Go!" Jesse commanded.

Adeline sheathed her dagger and climbed onto the windowsill. After a quick glance outside, she jumped. The impact stung her feet, and she quickly moved aside to avoid being hit.

Jesse and Caleb soared through the air and landed hard beside her, both managing to stay on their feet with Caleb still clinging to Jesse's backpack.

Heads popped out of the open window above as warriors shouted over one another. Ralock's unmistakable voice cut through the chaos. "Find them!"

Chapter Twenty-Nine

Hordes of Ralock's military swarmed the premises. Some were on horseback, others on foot. Angry shouts rumbled as Adeline and her friends rushed toward the trees, Jesse leading the way.

As they neared the thick tree line, Jesse came to a sudden stop. Caleb bumped into him but recovered his balance as Adeline halted beside them.

"Why did you stop?" she whispered, her chest pounding.

Jesse didn't need to answer.

Three hunters emerged from the trees, heading straight toward them with jagged swords. Their yellow eyes glowed against their painted faces as they marched in eerie unison, scanning the area.

Movement beyond the hunters caught Adeline's eye. More hunters and warriors combed the forest, making a ruckus as they trudged through the woods, slashing at anything that moved.

Adeline felt a sickening plunge in her stomach. "What do we do?"

"I know where we can hide," Caleb said in a rush. "Go to those cottages."

The sun started to descend as Jesse darted toward the brick cottages nestled against the forest's edge. There was a long row of them, each neglected and overwhelmed with weeds. Though they appeared deserted, Adeline noticed figures shifting behind the barred windows as she hurried past.

"Go to the last house," Caleb said, struggling to match Jesse's long strides.

The unkempt grass scratched at Adeline's ankles as she followed Caleb, moving away from the chaos.

They reached the last cottage tucked against the woods, and the rusted gate whined as they entered the backyard. Weeds dominated everything, including the brick walkway that led to another iron-barred door.

Jesse started toward it, but Caleb stopped him. "Hold on."

Bending over, Caleb grabbed one of the corner bricks on the path. It wiggled like a loose tooth before giving way, revealing a small key. He snatched it up and pulled Jesse toward the barred door, inserting the key into the first lock. It turned without a fight, granting access to the back door. Caleb quickly unlocked it and scurried inside with Jesse.

Adeline was right behind them. As soon as she stepped through, Caleb shut both doors and locked them, tucking the key into his pocket.

"You can let go of my backpack now," Jesse said, glancing back at Caleb. "They won't find us here."

Caleb let go, exhaustion claiming his bruised face. Without a word, he disappeared down the nearby hallway.

Jesse placed the flat of his blade against his palm until it lit up, removing his invisibility. He touched Adeline's arm before putting the sword away.

No longer glowing, Adeline glanced around the living area using what was left of the evening light. The musky odor was hard to ignore, as was the mismatched furniture. A velvet green couch clashed with the burgundy one beside it, joined by a tacky old recliner. She felt as if she'd stepped into an antique store.

"Who lives here?" she asked.

"No one," Jesse said, removing his weapons. "This place belonged to one of Caleb's friends."

Adeline lifted a brow. "What kind of friend?"

Jesse gave her a look she knew all too well. He wasn't going to tell her.

Rolling her eyes, Adeline pretended to be interested in the brick fireplace nestled between two dim hallways. She was curious about where they led, but was too tired to investigate. Sleep was the only thing on her mind. "How long are we going to stay here?"

"We'll sleep here tonight and leave in the morning," Jesse said, sinking into the recliner.

"Works for me."

Adeline leaned her bow against the wall before plopping down on the nearest couch. It wasn't overly comfortable, but she didn't care as she unbuckled her sheath and quiver, letting them drop to the floor. It felt good to get rid of the extra weight.

Sinking deeper into the cushions, she rubbed her aching neck as Caleb emerged from the hall. He brushed past her and collapsed onto the other couch. He looked depressed and completely drained as he stared at the ground.

"We're staying here tonight," Jesse said to Caleb.

Caleb didn't respond, nor did he acknowledge Jesse. He simply curled up on the velvet couch and closed his only working eye. Seconds later, he was out cold. Soft snores escaped from his swollen lips.

Concern rose in Adeline as she watched him sleep. He looked terrible. His injuries wouldn't heal overnight, no matter how much he slept.

"Thank you for helping me rescue Caleb." Jesse smiled at her.

"You're welcome," she said, returning his smile.

"Rest."

Adeline yawned, not bothering to cover her mouth, as she reached for a nearby pillow. She shifted into a more comfortable position. The moment her head hit the cushion, she was asleep.

***

Whispers stirred Adeline from her sleep. She pried open her tired eyes, disoriented. It took a moment for her to remember where she was.

Moonlight spilled in from the living room window, illuminating two figures seated in front of it. Their backs were to her, but she knew it was Caleb and Jesse. They kept their voices low as they looked out at the starry night. Adeline couldn't help but eavesdrop.

"I bet it was hard being here without Olivia," Jesse said, keeping his gaze ahead.

Caleb didn't respond right away. An uncomfortable silence passed before he replied, "How did you know this was Olivia's cottage?"

"I knew her. She was a wonderful woman."

Adeline didn't need to see Caleb's face to know he was upset. His tight posture gave it away, along with the heavy shift in the air.

"You're going to make it out of here, Caleb," Jesse said, glancing at him.

"I *was* out of here until I ran into you."

"You wouldn't have lasted a week with those wolves."

"You don't know that," Caleb hissed.

"They didn't need you anymore and were going to eat you."

Caleb mumbled something inaudible as he struggled to rise, grabbing the end table for support. He was clearly done talking. Hobbling back to the couch, he curled up again and closed his eye.

As Caleb drifted off, Adeline lay awake thinking about the mysterious woman named Olivia. Was she Caleb's girlfriend? Friend? Relative?

The questions came piling in.

What happened to her? Where did she go?

Olivia wasn't around, so there were only two possibilities. She either escaped the Dark Territory or died trying. Adeline hoped it wasn't the latter, but the growing pit in her stomach told her otherwise.

Chapter Thirty

A loud sound ripped Adeline from her deep slumber. She bolted upright, her heart slamming against her ribs. Panting, she darted quick glances around the room lit by the morning sun. She quickly found the source of the noise.

Caleb was sprawled on his back, snores rattling from his open mouth. One arm and leg dangled off the couch like dead weight. How was he sleeping like that?

Adeline dropped back onto her pillow. She shut her heavy eyes, trying to ignore the snores as her heart gradually slowed to a normal rhythm. Exhaustion pulsed through her temples and weighed down every inch of her body. Maybe she could get another hour of sleep.

The minutes ticked by, and Caleb's snores only grew louder, as if he was trying to annoy Adeline on purpose. She knew that wasn't true, but her irritation kept growing. She needed sleep, but she wasn't going to get any with him around.

Grabbing the pillow from under her head, Adeline threw it at Caleb.

It whacked his leg, jolting him awake. He jerked up, breathing hard. But when he saw the pillow, he groaned and flopped back down. "Leave me alone, Adeline."

"I would if you'd stop making so much noise," she said, using her arm as a pillow.

Jesse waltzed in from the hallway. "Good morning, sunshine."

The fresh scent of spring followed him as he wrung a towel through his damp hair. He was squeaky clean, rocking a fresh white tee and cargo pants.

Adeline sat up. "You took a shower?"

"Yep." He tossed the towel over the back of the recliner. "You can take one too if you want. I left the soap in there."

Adeline sprang to her feet, barely containing her excitement as she looked herself over. Her skin was stained with blood and dirt. So were her holey tank top and jean shorts. "Do you have any clean clothes that'll fit me?"

"No, but check the bedroom." Jesse pointed down the hall. "You'll find something that'll work."

Adeline was already heading down the hall when Jesse called out to her.

"You might need this." He held up a clean towel he'd pulled from his backpack.

Adeline turned and held out her hands.

Jesse grinned and rolled the towel into a ball. He pitched it like a baseball, and it hit her square in the chest.

She giggled. "Thanks."

Stiff and sore, she shuffled down the bare hall, hoping a warm shower would ease her aching muscles as she stepped into the bedroom.

The air was stale, and the room held nothing more than a bed and an antique dresser, both blanketed with dust.

Adeline went straight to the dresser. A single picture frame rested on top. She picked it up and blew away the dust, surprised to find a photo of a woman and a teenage boy, both wearing quiet grins.

The woman looked to be in her late thirties, with brown curls and large, chocolate-colored eyes. Her arm was wrapped around a tall teenager who looked just like her. They had to be related.

Adeline traced her finger along the picture. *Is this Olivia?*

She'd assumed Caleb's friend was their age. Maybe she was wrong. And who was the teenager? It definitely wasn't Caleb.

Returning the frame to the dresser, Adeline kept thinking about the anonymous faces as she opened the middle drawer. There wasn't much in there besides a couple pairs of socks and a leather belt. She grabbed some socks and checked another drawer. After a quick rummage, she found a pair of athletic shorts and a black T-shirt that looked to be her size. They had an old smell to them, but they were better than the ones she was wearing.

The dusty picture still occupied her thoughts as she left the bedroom and stepped into the bathroom. She flipped the switch. The single light bulb sputtered to life, buzzing as it lit the humid space. It desperately needed to be cleaned and disinfected, but Adeline was past the point of caring as she wiped the steam from the oval-shaped mirror.

A rush of heat rolled up her cheeks when she saw her reflection. Her messy bun was lopsided, and streaks of dirt coated her face. There was no avoiding the dark bruise on her cheek or the knot protruding from her forehead. It was the size of a golf ball and tender to the touch.

Pulling out her knotted bun, Adeline let her thick auburn hair fall in a crinkly mess down her back. Insecurity quickly gave way to laughter as she pulled a stick from the tangled strands. She couldn't get over how ridiculous she looked and could only imagine what Caleb and Jesse thought.

She did her best to detangle the mess, working her fingers through the knots. As she combed through her thick mane, she accidentally bumped the vanity. Something jarred in her pocket.

Frowning, Adeline pulled out the old pocket watch she'd found in the desert days ago. She'd forgotten all about it and was surprised that it hadn't fallen out during the chaotic journey.

She held up the golden timepiece. "I wonder who you belong to."

After a quick inspection, she placed it on the sink and turned on the shower. Hot water gushed from the showerhead, and she nearly squealed as steam filled the room. She undressed in a rush, tossing her soiled clothes into the corner. She didn't bother checking the temperature before stepping under the spray.

***

The hot shower did wonders for Adeline. She couldn't stop grinning as she breezed down the hallway, tossing her damp hair over her shoulder. The fresh scent of shampoo lingered around her as she entered the living room.

Jesse was reclining on the couch with his ankles crossed. An assortment of snacks was spread across the coffee table in front of him. Caleb was nowhere to be seen.

"How was it?" Jesse asked, pouring a handful of peanuts into his palm and popping them into his mouth.

"Amazing." Adeline grabbed a pack of cashews and plopped down next to him. "Where's Caleb?"

"In the other shower."

"Good." She tore open the packet. "He smelled awful."

"He wasn't the only one." Jesse elbowed her playfully.

Adeline shot him a disapproving look.

"You know I'm right." Jesse laughed.

Adeline's fake annoyance quickly dissolved into giggles. He was right. She'd smelled just as bad as Caleb. Maybe worse.

They ate their breakfast in comfortable silence, staring out the window that faced the forest. A light mist clung to the trees. It was more calming than spooky, nearly enough to make her forget they were deep in enemy territory.

Thinking about their escape had Adeline's stomach in knots. She didn't want to know the details, fearing it would only make things harder. Hopefully, they'd have an easier day and reach the cabin before dark.

Light thumps echoed from the other hallway, followed by the soft click of a closing door. Adeline turned to look but didn't see Caleb. He was probably changing in one of the bedrooms.

"Do you want anything else to eat?" Jesse asked.

"No, I'm good." Adeline tossed the empty wrapper onto the table.

Jesse began packing up the remaining snacks, and Adeline figured Caleb had already eaten.

"We'll have to head out soon." Jesse shifted items around in his bag to fit the rest of the food. "Will you get Caleb?"

"Where is he?" she asked, rising from the couch.

"His old bedroom," Jesse said, nodding toward the other hallway. "First door on your left."

Adeline blinked. "Wait. Caleb lived here? I thought this was his friend's house."

"It was, but he lived here too."

Before she could ask another question, Jesse's voice filled her thoughts. *"He'll tell you about Olivia when he's ready."*

"Why can't you tell me?"

Jesse gave her a look. "Go get Caleb."

With an eye roll, Adeline left Jesse and headed to the bedroom. The door was closed, so she knocked. "Caleb?"

"It's unlocked," came his muffled reply through the door.

Adeline pushed it open just in time to see Caleb tug a clean T-shirt over his head. It was too big for him. So were the gym shorts that hung past his knees.

Leaning against the doorframe, Adeline glanced around the small bedroom. It was just as plain as the other one. Nothing but the basics.

When she looked back at Caleb, he was staring at her with a look she couldn't decipher.

"What?" she asked.

"You look...uh...different with your hair down," he said as he sank into the mattress. "I didn't recognize you at first."

"I thought the same thing when I saw your shaved head."

He ran a hand through his buzz cut, his face darkening. "I don't remember them shaving it."

"It needed to be cut," Adeline said, stepping into the room and sitting beside him. "It looks a lot better now."

"If you say so." His eyes dropped to his lap.

Just looking at him made her heart ache. His face was swollen and badly bruised, especially around his right eye. Still, he looked better now that he'd showered. And he smelled better too. "How's your eye?"

"It's okay." He shrugged. "I just wish I could see out of it."

"I bet Jesse has something that could help." She slowly pushed herself up. "I'll go check."

Adeline slipped out of the room and returned a few minutes later with a small metal tin. She held it up. "Found something."

The mattress dipped slightly as she sat next to Caleb and faced him.

"What is it?" he asked, refusing to look at her.

"No idea," she said with a shrug. "Jesse said it would help."

Caleb shifted uncomfortably. "I don't need it."

"Don't be a baby." She twisted the lid off, releasing a strong herbal smell. "It'll only take a second."

"I don't want it."

"Why not?" she asked, pushing down her own frustration. "It'll help your eye heal faster."

Caleb was silent, staring at his bruised knuckles. Seconds of silence stretched on before he spoke again. "I don't want you looking at my face."

"Why? I've already seen it."

"I saw my reflection," he said, his voice dropping to a whisper. "I look like a monster."

A pang of sorrow stirred in Adeline. "You're not a monster, Caleb," she said softly. "You're injured."

Silence settled over them once more. He hung his head and swallowed hard, his Adam's apple bobbing. He wouldn't look at her.

"Let me help you," she said, breaking the silence.

When he didn't move, Adeline reached out and gently took his chin, turning his face toward her. Pain and shame clouded his green eye as he lifted it to hers.

His physical injuries were obvious, but she saw something deeper. Like she was viewing the torment of his soul. It was heartbreaking. She pretended not to notice and focused on his other eye.

Her chest tightened. It was worse than she'd thought.

The entire eye was triple in size, completely discolored, and puffy. She worried he might lose his vision.

Keeping her thoughts to herself, Adeline tucked her damp hair behind her ears and dabbed the pad of her finger into the clear paste. Caleb winced as she applied it to his eye. She tried to be gentle, but Caleb groaned, fisting his hands in his lap.

After fully medicating his eye, she treated the rest of his face. He flinched and moaned with each touch, struggling to sit still. At least he wasn't yelling at her.

"Hopefully, this stuff works." She closed the tin and offered a small smile. "If not, at least you smell nice."

Caleb didn't smile back as he eased himself to the edge of the bed. Pain contorted his face as he slowly stood.

A small note slipped from his pocket and landed on the bed next to Adeline.

"What's this?" she asked, picking it up.

The paper was worn and crinkled, folded into a square no bigger than her palm. *Little Wilder* was written on it in faded letters. She ran her finger over the black ink. "Who's Little Wilder?"

Caleb snatched the note from her and shoved it back into his pocket. "It was the nickname my grandfather gave me."

"Why?"

"My last name is Wilder."

"Wilder?" Adeline sat up straighter. "You're a Wilder?"

"Yeah..."

"The house I live in used to be owned by Mr. Wilder."

He stood immobile. "You live on Pivotal Point Road?"

"Yes!" she exclaimed. "I moved there almost a year ago."

Caleb's jaw dropped. "I grew up there with my grandfather."

"No way!" Adeline launched to her feet. "Are you serious?"

"Yes."

"This is insane." She ran her hands through her auburn hair. "Your family owns the gated woods behind my backyard, right?"

"Well, technically I do," he said, shifting his weight. "I'm the only one left."

"You don't have any family?" she asked, her grin slipping away. "No siblings, parents, or relatives?"

"No." Caleb's mouth tightened. "I don't have anyone."

Tears pricked Adeline's eyes as she thought about Dad. Losing him had been hard. She couldn't imagine losing her entire family. "I'm really sorry, Caleb."

Caleb stuck his hands in his pockets, avoiding her gaze. "How did you find this realm? My family kept it a secret for generations."

"I found the key to the gate."

Caleb looked confused. "Where?"

"In that old shed."

"I thought I had the only key." He shook his head, cracking a tiny grin. "Grandpa must've hidden a spare."

Adeline was still trying to make sense of everything. She'd often thought of the Wilder family, even dreamed of meeting them one day. It never crossed her mind that Caleb might be one of them. "I'm glad he did; my whole life is better because of it," she said with a quiet sincerity. "We should go. Jesse's waiting for us."

The old pocket watch knocked against Adeline's thigh as she went to leave. It was moving around too much in her gym shorts. Fearing it might fall out, she pulled it from her pocket so she could stick it in Jesse's backpack.

"What is that?" Caleb asked.

"It's just an old watch I found in the desert."

"Let me see it." He held out his hand.

Adeline handed it over, surprised by his insistence.

Caleb looked like he'd seen a ghost as he flipped it over. "How is this possible?"

"What do you mean?"

"This was my grandfather's pocket watch." He ran his thumb over the engraved *W* on the case. "I got it after he died."

"Really?"

"Yeah," Caleb said, still staring at the golden timepiece. "I lost it in the desert; I never thought I'd see it again."

Adeline's mind reeled. The Red-Rock Region was vast, filled with endless nooks and crannies. The odds of her finding his pocket watch were slim to none. It was as if she were destined to find it. Just like she was destined to meet him.

"Thank you," Caleb said, barely getting the words out. "You have no idea how much this means to me."

"You're welcome." Adeline gave a small nod. "I'm glad it's back where it belongs."

Caleb clutched it tightly and pressed it to his chest. "Me too."

Chapter Thirty-One

Heavy, humid air clung to the morning as Adeline and her friends left the cottage and made their way to the woods. It was still early, but the city was wide awake and just as noisy as the day before. Shouts and high-pitched screams pierced the air as the military continued their hunt for Adeline and Caleb.

Jesse was the first to enter the forest, hustling away from the noise and mountain range with Caleb clinging to his backpack. A faint white light surrounded them as Adeline followed. Jesse used his body to plow through the thick, thorny briars and tangled undergrowth. Thorns ripped his shirt and lashed his arms, but he kept going, carving a makeshift path for her and Caleb.

Some of the thorns whipped back, scratching Adeline as she pressed on. Within minutes, sweat coated her skin, and she was thankful she'd tied her hair up before they'd left.

The farther they went, the worse it got.

Gnats swarmed her face as she trudged through the thick forest, her clothes now soaked in sweat. She'd tripped and untangled her bow so many times, she stopped counting.

When will this nightmare be over? She shoved a branch out of her way.

By the time she spotted a dirt path ahead, her calves were on fire. Voices boomed in the distance, though no one was in sight as they neared the well-maintained trail. Jesse stopped just short of it, looking both ways.

Caleb trembled. "I think we're close to the red zone."

"We're in it," Jesse said, sweat dripping from his beard.

Caleb gulped as he scanned the treetops. "We have to avoid the watchtowers. Look, there's one."

Caleb pointed ahead. Following his finger, Adeline squinted through the canopy until she spotted it. The watchtower blended so well with the forest, she hadn't noticed it at first. A metal ladder climbed a thick tree trunk, leading to a small platform that looked more like a hunting stand than a tower. A hunter stood there, bow in hand, his camouflaged face blank as he surveyed the area.

"This road will take us to the safe part of the forest," Jesse said, watching the hunter.

A shiver ran through Adeline as she glanced down the man-made trail. It stretched in a straight line as far as she could see, like the trees had been cleared with heavy machinery. Traveling would be much easier and faster.

Arguing reached her ears. Moments later, two warriors came out of the trees and onto the path. One was male, the other female, both moving with purpose. Their black combat boots pounded the ground as they strode away from the watchtower without sparing a glance at the hunter.

"This is madness," the male warrior said, his battle-ax bouncing at his hip. "We've been searching all night—and nothing!"

"Shut up." The woman whacked the side of his head. "Do you want the master to hear you?"

"You know I'm right," he said. "The boy's tracker isn't working; he's probably long gone by now."

"Keep your opinions to yourself," she growled, resting a hand on her sheathed dagger as she walked. "I won't be punished because of your mouth."

He continued to argue his point as they walked along the trail, eventually disappearing in the distance.

Jesse glanced back at Caleb. "Let's move."

Keeping his eyes on the hunter, Jesse crawled out of the briars with Caleb close behind. Caleb wasn't nearly as bloody as Jesse, but he did have some tears in his clothes and a few scrapes.

They reached the road and shifted over to make room for Adeline. Thorns tore at her skin, but she persevered, planting one foot on the trail. As she tugged the other free, her sneaker got caught.

She lost her balance, but Caleb caught her arm and steadied her.

The hunter snapped his head in their direction. Neither of them moved as his yellow eyes slowly glided over the woods, unblinking.

After what felt like an eternity, he looked away and resumed his watch.

Glancing back, Jesse pressed a finger to his lips before pointing down the road. Terror gripped Adeline. They were going to walk right past the guard tower.

Caleb shook his head repeatedly, but that didn't stop Jesse from tiptoeing toward the armed hunter. With no other choice, Caleb followed.

Fear crawled along Adeline's back as she plucked a thorn from her shin and hurried after them. Her heart picked up speed the closer they got to the hunter. He stood like a statue, his dark green armor blending perfectly with the trees. No wonder they dressed that way.

Jesse and Caleb successfully snuck past the hunter. Adeline was next.

Holding her breath, Adeline feared the hunter might hear her pounding heart as she crept forward, careful not to make a sound. The guard tower creaked overhead as he shifted his weight, scanning the forest. She inched by him, the soft dirt muting her steps. Her lungs burned for air, but she didn't dare breathe until she was well beyond his line of sight.

Adeline reached her friends, who were waiting for her, and they resumed their journey. The wind whispered through the dense trees, causing the leaves to rustle and the branches to sway. Every creak and groan in the forest sharpened her unease.

Walking beside Jesse, she noticed weariness clouding his face. It wasn't just exhaustion; he was troubled by something. She could sense it.

"What's wrong?" she whispered.

Jesse glanced her way. His mouth opened, then shut, as if he was struggling to find the right words. Then his voice entered her mind.

"I need you to promise me something."

Adeline didn't like the sound of that. *"Okay."*

"Whatever happens, I need you and Caleb to go to the cabin and stay there."

She shot him a startled look, her mind spinning as they walked. *"What's going to happen?"*

He looked at her. *"Promise me."*

Sorrow surfaced in his emerald eyes, catching her off guard. *"You're scaring me."*

"Promise me, Addie."

Rustling in the nearby forest brought an abrupt end to their conversation.

A pack of wild dogs barreled out of the woods, heading straight toward them. They were tall and thin like greyhounds, but aggressive like rabid animals. Their paws pounded into the dirt as they ran full speed, barking ferociously.

Jesse leaped into the woods with Caleb still clinging to his backpack. Adeline jumped the opposite way, a bush breaking her fall. Limbs jabbed into her as the dogs blazed by. Their snarls and howls faded within seconds.

Adeline climbed out of the bush and quickly checked her bow. Seeing no damage, she crossed the road to find Jesse and Caleb.

There wasn't as much undergrowth in that section of the forest, and Adeline easily found Jesse. He was on his feet, wiping the dirt from his shirt. A quick glance behind him caused her to freeze. Caleb wasn't there.

"Where's Caleb?" she asked, a tremble threading through her voice.

"I'm over here."

Several yards away, Caleb rose from the dirt, smoke curling off his body. Leaves and grime clung to him. He'd clearly rolled several times.

Caleb limped toward them, his face etched with fear.

"Don't move!" Jesse threw up a hand.

Snap!

A rope whipped around Caleb's ankle and jerked him into the air. He dangled upside down, thrashing violently.

"Help me!" he cried.

Adeline's eyes darted up to the tree. "How do we get him down?" she asked, trying to stay calm. "The rope's too high!"

Jesse snatched an arrow from his quiver and nocked it against the bowstring. His muscles flexed as he took aim. Then he released.

The arrow sliced clean through the center of the rope.

Yelping, Caleb flailed as he dropped headfirst. Jesse lunged forward, letting his bow fall with a clatter. He caught Caleb mid-fall and set him down. Smoke rose from his skin as he worked quickly to untangle the rope from Caleb's ankle.

A distant shout pierced the trees. Someone must've heard them.

Loading her bow, Adeline searched the forest while Jesse helped Caleb to his feet.

"What do we do?" she asked, her pulse quickening.

"We're taking the road." Jesse picked up his bow. "There are too many traps in here."

Movement flickered behind Jesse and Caleb—fast and quiet. Adeline's gaze locked onto a hunter, barely visible beside a towering pine. He stood perfectly still, his bow already drawn.

Caleb's head was his target.

"Duck!" Adeline shouted, swinging her bow toward the threat.

Jesse hit the dirt, dragging Caleb with him right as Adeline released her arrow. It zipped over their heads and struck the hunter square in the face. He fell to the ground, dead.

But he wasn't alone.

Shadows moved between the trees. More were coming.

"Run," Jesse said, already loading his bow. "I'll catch up."

He loosed an arrow, catching a second hunter in the throat as Caleb scrambled to his feet and bolted toward the road. Adeline took off after him, easily catching up.

Adrenaline kicked in, and she tore down the path. Caleb's breathing was labored and his strides irregular, but he kept up with her even though he couldn't see her. She purposely left a wide gap between them so he wouldn't accidentally bump into her.

"They're on the trail!" a loud voice boomed behind them.

Adeline glanced back and saw Jesse dash onto the road. He sprinted after them, no longer wearing his backpack. All he had were his weapons.

Three hunters leaped onto the path, bows drawn. They fired.

Jesse ducked and weaved, dodging each one by inches. While the enemy reloaded, he spun, loaded his bow, and unleashed a rapid barrage of arrows.

Wham! Wham! Wham!

Each arrow struck its mark, slamming into the hunters' chests. They crumbled where they stood, blood pouring into the dirt.

With the hunters down, Jesse chased after Adeline and Caleb.

"Keep going!" Jesse said, motioning them forward with a sharp wave.

Panting, Adeline pushed herself harder. Her skin prickled with heat as she pumped her arms, bow in hand. Every muscle screamed with fatigue, but she couldn't stop now.

Caleb was still with her, but not for long. He staggered to a halt, wheezing for air. "I can't run anymore."

"You have to." Adeline stopped, her own breathing rough.

"I can't."

"Come on, Caleb." Jesse caught up to them. "We've got to go."

"Go without me."

"We're not leaving you." Jesse gripped his arm, urging him forward.

Caleb shook his arm free as the enemy's shouts intensified. They would be there soon.

Jesse scratched his beard, his eyes darting across the forest in search of a solution. Suddenly, his expression lit up. He placed two fingers on his lips and let out a loud burst of whistles. At once, the forest came alive as a flurry of hidden birds repeated the tune.

"What are you doing?" Adeline asked, wincing as her ears rang.

"Calling the horses," Jesse said, his chest rising and falling rapidly.

The birds' calls bounced through the trees, gradually fading until the forest fell quiet again.

Reassurance washed through Adeline as she took measured breaths. She hadn't thought of that. It would take some time for Angela and Regal to reach them, but knowing they were on their way brought her comfort.

Galloping filled the air, and Adeline nearly leaped for joy. She spun in a circle, searching for them, but her excitement quickly turned to fear as five black stallions emerged from the trees, each ridden by a warrior. Their dark armor glinted in the sun as they formed a tight line across the road.

There was no way through.

Adeline scrambled for an escape plan, but nothing came to mind. They couldn't outrun the horses, and the forest was full of hidden snares.

Reality sank in.

They were trapped.

Chapter Thirty-Two

Fear-stricken, Adeline fumbled to load her bow. Her limbs wouldn't obey as she stared at the enemy. They weren't overly close, but close enough for her to make out their faces. She sized each one up, but her stomach plummeted when her eyes landed on the man in the center.

It wasn't a warrior. It was Ralock.

He was dressed like the others, a sword strapped across his back.

"I'm a bit surprised to see you here, Jesse." Ralock dismounted and stood before his small army. His cold eyes shifted to Caleb, who instinctively stepped back. "Especially with one of my followers."

Jesse stepped in front of Caleb. "He doesn't belong to you anymore."

"Is that so?" Ralock lifted a dark brow. "Last time I checked, he had *my* tattoo."

"What tattoo?"

Ralock snapped his gaze to Caleb's forearm. A perplexed look crossed his striking features. It quickly vanished, replaced by an arrogant smirk. "It doesn't matter. I'll still kill the boy."

Ralock threw back his head with a wicked laugh and raised his hands skyward. The clouds swirled and churned as they darkened. A powerful gust of wind hit the trees, bending branches and rattling leaves as thunder growled overhead.

"What do we do, Jesse?" Adeline asked as the wind tore at her hair, pulling a few strands free.

"We fight." Jesse reached for another arrow but touched nothing but air. His quiver was empty.

"You're out of arrows."

"Good thing I have a sword." Jesse tossed his useless bow into the woods and unsheathed his long blade.

Adeline smelled the rain before it fell. A few scattered drops pattered against the earth, quickly building into a steady drizzle. Raindrops tapped against the warriors' armor as they dismounted their stallions and drew their weapons. They slapped their horses' backsides, making them rear before bolting into the woods.

"This is going to be fun," Ralock said above the storm as he turned to his warriors. "Kill the boy, but leave Jesse for me."

Thunder cracked above as the warriors advanced. Ralock stayed back, unmoved in the rain. He crossed his arms, haughtiness plastered across his face.

"They can't see you; aim for their necks," Jesse said in her mind.

With trembling hands, Adeline loaded her bow. Heavy raindrops pelted her skin as she raised the weapon, debating which warrior to shoot first. They were all bigger than her, so she aimed for the brawniest of the group.

Wham!

The bulky man shrieked, clawing at the arrow lodged in his neck. Blood gushed through his fingers as he fell to his knees.

"What the—" Ralock reached over his shoulder and drew his sword, holding the jagged black blade out defensively as he scanned the area.

Confusion rippled through the warriors. They huddled together, their eyes darting as they searched for the unseen assailant, scanning the green forest high and low.

Adeline fired again. The arrow whipped past the tallest warrior, slicing his ear. He released an angry shout as he clutched the bloody wound.

Adeline reloaded her bow, her heartbeat pounding in her temples as she aimed at the same warrior. Her muscles screamed for relief, but she blocked out the pain until she locked in her aim. With a slow breath, she loosed the arrow.

The arrow sliced through the air and slammed into the warrior's mouth. Blood sprayed the others as he slumped to the earth, never to rise again.

Her aim was a little off, but at least she had killed him.

"Bigsby is here," Ralock roared, his face darkening with rage.

Chills slid down her spine as she grabbed another arrow and nocked it. Two warriors remained.

Twigs snapping reached her ears, growing louder by the second. A quick glance into the trees made her chest tighten. Slow-moving figures crept through the woods, drawing closer. She caught glimpses of dark green armor.

"Hunters are coming." Jesse twirled his sword once, then settled into a fighter's stance. *"Kill them. I'll take care of the others."*

Being hidden from the outside world gave Adeline the upper hand, but it didn't calm her raging heart. Focusing on the woods, she launched arrows at the advancing hunters. It was hard to aim with so many trees, but she hit some of them. Their agonizing groans were heard over the rumbling storm.

The remaining hunters no longer cared about being stealthy. They emerged from the woods onto the trail one by one, weapons drawn, and raced toward Jesse as he battled the warriors. Their obliviousness to Adeline made them easy targets. She killed each one with a single arrow to the chest.

When no more hunters appeared, she turned around as Jesse decapitated the last warrior. The man's head hit the ground, bouncing off another fallen warrior, while his lifeless body slumped at Jesse's feet. Blood spattered his boots as he stood tall, his sword dripping red as he pointed it at Ralock.

"You don't scare me," Ralock hissed as water dripped from his short black hair.

He strutted toward Jesse, his nostrils flaring as his combat boots squished into the wet earth. Jesse stepped over the dead warrior and met him halfway. He struck first, but Ralock blocked the blow with his blade.

Sparks flew as metal clanged against metal. The fight had officially begun.

Adeline snatched an arrow from her quiver, ready to help. As she loaded her bow, a sudden blow struck her back. She faltered but caught herself, then spun around and came face-to-face with a hunter who had accidentally run into her. He looked just as stunned, his yellow eyes wide with shock.

With the arrow still in hand, Adeline lunged and drove the point into the hunter's neck. She shoved him hard, sending him crashing backward. His head slammed into the dirt, and he lay motionless, the arrow jutting from his neck.

Caleb ran up to Adeline, visibly shaking. "Are you okay?"

"Yeah," she said, wiping the blood from her face. "Are you?"

Caleb nodded, his eyes drifting back to the battle between Jesse and Ralock.

Rain pelted against them as the two men grunted and roared with every clash. Ralock's blade looked like death as he swung at Jesse. Jesse jumped back, deflecting his move, before countering with one of his own. They went back and forth, mirroring one another as if performing a dance. It was captivating to watch.

Snapping out of her stupor, Adeline reached over her head for another arrow. She only had a few left. "We need to help Jesse."

"Adeline." Caleb pointed behind her, his finger trembling. "We've got a problem."

Thunder cracked above as Adeline spun around. A group of warriors marched their way. The men and women looked as deadly as the weapons they carried.

Adeline was tempted to turn herself and Caleb invisible, but that wouldn't work. She couldn't aim straight with him clinging to her. She thought about just turning invisible herself, but quickly dismissed it. The warriors would go after Caleb, and she wasn't willing to risk his safety.

"Get behind me," Adeline said, nocking her arrow.

"There are too many of them." Caleb dropped to his knees, frantically searching a fallen hunter's pockets. He stood a moment later with a fistful of throwing knives. "I can help you."

Flashbacks whipped through her mind as she looked at the eerie black blades. Nothing in her wanted him to use them, but she needed help. Hopefully, he could aim with only one working eye.

"Don't hold on to those for too long," Adeline warned, lifting her bow toward the approaching army. "I don't want to fight you too."

"Wasn't planning on it."

Caleb wound back his arm and hurled the knife. It struck the lead warrior's skull like a bullet. The man's heavy body toppled backward, crashing into the warrior behind him.

Adeline hadn't expected that, but she quickly recovered from the shock. There was no time to praise him. She let her arrow fly.

The warrior collapsed on impact, and the others broke into a sprint. Their lack of bows and arrows left them at a serious disadvantage.

Rain poured down as Adeline and Caleb fought side by side. The warriors dropped like flies, with Caleb killing the majority of them.

When the last one fell, Adeline lowered her bow, her chest heaving. She scanned the shadowed forest but saw nothing. That only made her more uneasy. More were bound to come.

"Where are the horses?" Caleb asked, breathless.

"I don't know." Adeline swiped the rain from her eyes. "They should be here soon."

Scuffling and grunts pulled her focus back to the fight between Jesse and Ralock. They were punching one another, their swords lying in the mud.

Lightning cracked across the sky as Jesse landed a left hook to Ralock's jaw. His head snapped back as he stumbled, his boots sloshing through the muck, but he recovered quickly and blocked the next punch.

"Look!" Caleb pointed down the path. "The horses!"

Relief bloomed in Adeline as Angela and Regal galloped toward them, splashing through the puddles. Their majestic manes flapped in the wind.

While she waited, Adeline grabbed her final arrow and loaded her bow.

It was time to kill Ralock once and for all.

Her muscles burned as she pulled back the tight string, aiming it at Ralock. He was still blocking and throwing punches at Jesse, making it hard to get a clean shot. Then he stopped, his back turned.

Gotcha.

Adeline locked aim. The forest fell silent around her as she released her fingers, the arrow whistling toward Ralock's unprotected back.

It was the perfect shot.

Just as the arrow was about to pierce Ralock's armor, he grabbed Jesse's shoulders and switched places with him.

Adeline's eyes widened in horror as her arrow struck Jesse square in the back.

Jesse sagged forward, one hand clutching the arrow sticking out of his chest. He fought for air as he looked back at her. "Go!" he shouted.

Before she could move, Ralock drove his sword through Jesse's torso. The blade burst through his back. Time seemed to slow as his body slumped and fell to the muddy earth.

"*No!*" A scream ripped from Adeline's throat as she dropped her bow and sprinted toward him.

But Regal slammed in front of her, blocking her path. The force of the impact sent her stumbling back a step.

"Move!" she cried, trying to shove past him.

The stallion didn't flinch. With a savage cry, he reared, flailing his hooves as Ralock stalked toward them, his sword still dripping with Jesse's blood.

Angela appeared behind her, Caleb already in the saddle. "We have to go!" Caleb shouted, grabbing Adeline's arm and trying to pull her up.

"We can't leave him!" she sobbed, clawing at his grip.

"He's dead!" Caleb yanked her harder. "We will be too if we don't leave now!"

Tears poured down Adeline's face as his words struck like a blade. Jesse was gone. She'd killed him.

"Adeline!" Caleb shouted again, panic in his voice.

Regal let out a piercing cry and charged. His hooves thundered through the mud as he barreled toward Ralock. At the last second, Ralock dodged him, veering to the side. But the sudden attack shattered his focus, forcing him to turn his attention to the raging stallion.

Raindrops streaked down Adeline's cheeks as she looked up at Caleb. His mouth moved, urgent and pleading, but all she heard was the howl of the wind as he tugged her arm.

At last, the severity of the situation sank in. Caleb was right. They'd die too if they didn't leave immediately.

She grabbed Caleb's arm, allowing him to haul her into the saddle. He threw an arm around her waist before kicking his heels into Angela.

Angela reared, then bolted.

The sudden jolt nearly threw Adeline off, but Caleb held her against his scrawny chest as they bounced in the saddle.

She looked back as a crack of thunder rattled her bones. Another cry tore from her throat.

Regal reared again, throwing himself into the swarm of warriors spilling from the trees. He kicked and struck with lethal force, guarding Jesse's body with unrelenting loyalty.

Adeline's heart shattered as she watched him fight alone beside Jesse's fallen form.

More enemies surged forward, but Regal didn't falter.

Her screams turned to sobs as Angela bolted down the trail, hooves pounding like war drums. They didn't slow until the path curved deep into the forest, the storm and slaughter lost behind the veil of trees.

The wind stilled, and the downpour faded to a light drizzle. The sudden shift in weather confirmed they were no longer in the Dark Territory.

Raindrops slipped from the branches as Angela slowed to a gentle trot. They weaved from path to path, fog clinging to the forest. Adeline's cries faded to silence, her body limp as she leaned against Caleb. He hadn't said a word, but his arms stayed around her.

Heartache overwhelmed Adeline as she gazed ahead. The pain was unbearable. Just like when Dad died, only heavier. Guilt wrapped around her like chains. She wished she'd died with Jesse.

"I'm sorry, Adeline," Caleb said, his voice barely above a whisper.

Adeline's bottom lip quivered. "I killed him."

"You didn't mean to. It was an accident."

"He's still dead."

Silence fell between them as Angela shifted onto another quiet path. A songbird darted through the branches as the rain picked up. Adeline listened to the soft patter of raindrops on the leaves, her thoughts drifting to Godfrey and Henry.

How was she supposed to face them? Especially Godfrey. She'd killed his son.

Terror and guilt pierced her. How could they ever forgive her?

The ache in her heart deepened. She couldn't lose them too. Life wouldn't be worth living without them.

Regal came to mind. Was he still alive? Or had he fallen beside Jesse?

Tears welled in her eyes again as Angela moved through the last line of trees. A sinking feeling took hold when she saw the cabin. No smoke curled from the chimney, and all the lights were out. Godfrey and Henry weren't home.

A small wave of relief washed over her as Angela trotted around the flowerbeds toward the front porch. She wasn't ready to face them. Not yet.

Angela stopped by the steps. Every muscle throbbed as Adeline slid off the saddle, landing hard in the wet grass. Another round of tears rolled down her cheeks as she dragged herself inside the cabin.

The warmth felt good against her chilled skin, but it did nothing for the hollow ache in her soul. She stood there, soaked, scanning the quiet space.

Jesse would never walk through that door again.

He was gone forever.

Adeline covered her face with trembling hands and wept. Empty sobs broke through as she shook uncontrollably, her heart shattering into a million pieces.

She heard the door close behind her and assumed Caleb had left. There was no reason for him to stay.

"Let's take off your weapons and get you warmed up," Caleb said gently from behind her.

Adeline lowered her hands and turned to him. "Why are you still here? Ralock can't track you anymore. You can go wherever you want."

"I'm not leaving you like this."

Adeline searched his bruised face for a long moment. He was hard to read, but she was almost certain she saw a flicker of compassion in his weary stare. Slowly, she dropped her gaze to her soaked shoes. Deep down, she was glad he was there. She didn't want to be alone.

Numbness settled over Adeline as she wiped her eyes again. Now that the tears were gone, exhaustion crept in. Her eyelids were hot and her throat raw as she fidgeted with her sheath. The leather was wet, making it hard to unbuckle.

Caleb stepped forward silently. He unfastened it on the first try, and the sheath dropped to the floor with a light thud.

Grateful to be free from its weight, Adeline unbuckled her empty quiver and tossed it against the wall.

"You're shivering," Caleb said, looking her over with concern. "I'll make us a fire."

Adeline didn't move. She hugged her arms tightly, staring at the puddle forming at her feet.

"Come on." Caleb took a step toward the couches.

Adeline remained frozen.

He exhaled, his hand drifting up to his shaved head before falling away. An uncomfortable expression crossed his face as he reached out and gently took hold of her arm.

Adeline let him guide her to the fireplace. The leather felt like ice as she sank into the familiar seat, water dripping from her hair.

Caleb placed a blanket over her, then went to build a fire. He stacked the wood and struck a match. A fire ignited, casting warm light across the room.

The orange glow followed Caleb as he sank into the opposite couch, pulling a blanket around his shoulders like a cape. He looked deep in thought as he watched the fire, the smell of birch wood permeating the air.

Adeline kicked off her soggy shoes and tugged the blanket to her chin, letting the warmth seep into her chilled bones. Jesse's absence was overwhelming, pressing in from every corner like a nightmare she couldn't escape. Fresh tears slipped free as she forced him from her thoughts. It was too painful.

She shifted, sinking deeper into the couch until her head met the pillow. The cushion cradled her, soft and comforting, but it couldn't ease the hollowness in her chest.

The crackle of the flames blurred into the rhythm of rain pattering softly against the roof. Her eyelids burned, threatening to close. She tried to resist, terrified of seeing Jesse die again the moment she surrendered to sleep. At last, her body gave in, and she drifted into darkness.

Chapter Thirty-Three

Adeline eased out of sleep, a steady throb pulsing in her temples. Her body felt heavy as she pushed herself upright, every muscle sore. Morning light spilled through the windows, painting the cabin in a warm glow. The fire had burned down to nothing but ash.

She glanced toward the other couch, and her heart sank. It was empty. The blanket was still there, rumpled at one end, but Caleb was gone.

He hadn't even said goodbye.

She rubbed her tired eyes, swallowing the lump in her throat. Maybe it was better that way. He wasn't her responsibility anymore.

Dragging herself to the bathroom, she peeled off her bloody clothes and stepped into the shower. She stood beneath the stream, numb, letting the water wash over her without feeling it. The memory of Jesse's death surfaced, and the numbness shattered. Sobs tore loose, her tears vanishing into the water. She wept until she had nothing left.

Eventually, she shut off the shower and wandered into the connecting bedroom, her limbs heavy with fatigue. Slipping into loungewear, she felt her soreness reawaken as her arms slid into the long sleeves with sluggish motions. Even standing felt like a chore.

Adeline brushed her damp hair behind her ears and lifted her gaze to the mirror. Bruises stood out against her pale skin, dark and unforgiving, and her eyes were swollen from crying. She barely recognized the girl staring back at her.

For a fleeting moment, she thought about going back to her world, leaving the cabin, and avoiding Godfrey and Henry. But the bruises made that impossible.

Her family would ask too many questions. Questions she couldn't answer. She was stuck there until they healed.

She shuffled from the bedroom and into the hallway, her bare feet cold on the wooden floor. The smell of coffee met her before she reached the kitchen, freezing her in place. Godfrey and Henry. They were back.

Wild panic stole her breath. She wasn't ready; she couldn't face them, not after what she'd done. They already knew; she was certain of it. But that only made things worse. Would they banish her from the cabin? Hate her forever? The thought nearly broke her, leaving her trembling in the hall. Yet there was no avoiding it.

Putting one foot in front of the other, Adeline exhaled slowly and entered the kitchen. A pot of coffee steamed on the counter, and beside it sat a plate of pastries. She didn't see anyone until she looked toward the living room.

She froze.

It wasn't Godfrey or Henry. It was Caleb.

He sat on the couch, a mug cupped between his hands. His face was still marred with bruises, his eyes ringed in black, but he was dressed in clean clothes that actually fit him.

Relief seeped into her as she took a slow breath. He was still there.

"Hey," Caleb said, his voice low.

"Hi." Adeline hugged herself, her heartbeat slowing. "I thought you'd left."

"You were still asleep when I got up, so I took a shower."

She nodded, her gaze dropping to her feet. "How are you feeling?"

"About the same," he said. "You?"

Adeline shrugged, holding back tears.

Silence stretched between them, weighted and thick with what neither dared to say.

"I made some coffee," Caleb said, gesturing toward the kitchen. "And there are pastries, if you want one."

Adeline skipped the coffee and grabbed a pastry instead. Carrying it into the living room, she sat on the opposite couch, picking at the flaky crust. One bite was all she managed before abandoning it on the end table.

"I'll stay here with you until Godfrey and Henry get back." Caleb's voice cut gently through the quiet.

Adeline blinked in surprise. "You know Godfrey as well?"

"Yeah." He winced as he readjusted on the couch. "I used to come here all the time."

"What happened?"

He hesitated. "It's a long story."

Adeline's throat tightened as her thoughts edged back toward Jesse and everything she had lost. She clenched her hands in her lap. She couldn't go there again. Maybe Caleb's story would be the distraction she needed.

"I have time," she said softly.

Caleb stared into his coffee. "You're not going to like it."

"I'll be the judge of that." She tucked her feet beneath her as she leaned into the armrest, bracing herself for the story she'd been waiting to hear.

Caleb shifted, rubbing the back of his neck. For a long time, he didn't speak. Then he looked at her, his good eye filled with worry and sadness.

"Okay," he said, releasing a long breath. "I'll start from the beginning."

Adeline sat still, her chest thumping. This was it. Caleb was finally going to tell his story.

Thank You for Reading!

If you enjoyed this story, please consider leaving a quick review. Whether it's on Amazon, Goodreads, or wherever you picked up this book, your honest review makes a big difference. It doesn't have to be long—just a few words can help other readers discover this book. Thank you for being a part of this adventure. I can't wait to share more with you soon! If you'd like to be the first to hear about new releases and special offers, visit www.elizabethmowery.com to sign up for my newsletter.

ACKNOWLEDGEMENTS

First and foremost, I want to give thanks to God. Without You, none of this would be possible. You gave me the spark of inspiration, the strength to keep going, and the reminder that this story was never just for me. Thank You for guiding me every step of the way.

To my incredible husband, Adam. You continue to be my biggest supporter. You've cheered me on through the countless hours poured into this story, endless edits, and moments of exhaustion. Your encouragement and belief in me have carried me through, and I couldn't imagine doing this without you.

To all my editors, family, and friends—your feedback and encouragement helped shape this story into what it is today. I deeply appreciate the time, effort, and honesty you poured into this book. You've made it stronger, richer, and better than I could have ever imagined on my own.

And finally, to you, dear reader. Thank you for coming back for book two in Adeline's journey. Your support means the world to me. I hope this story has captivated you, and I can't wait to share what comes next.

ABOUT THE AUTHOR

Elizabeth Mowery is an avid writer who has a passion for creating exciting stories that capture the imagination of her readers. She lives in the foothills of North Carolina, where she loves spending time with her family and friends. When she isn't writing, she can be found enjoying the simple pleasures in life—a hot cup of coffee, the fresh air of the outdoors, and a good book. Connect with her at www.elizabethmowery.com

9 798990 015128